THIS BOOK IS THE SOLE PROPERTY OF:

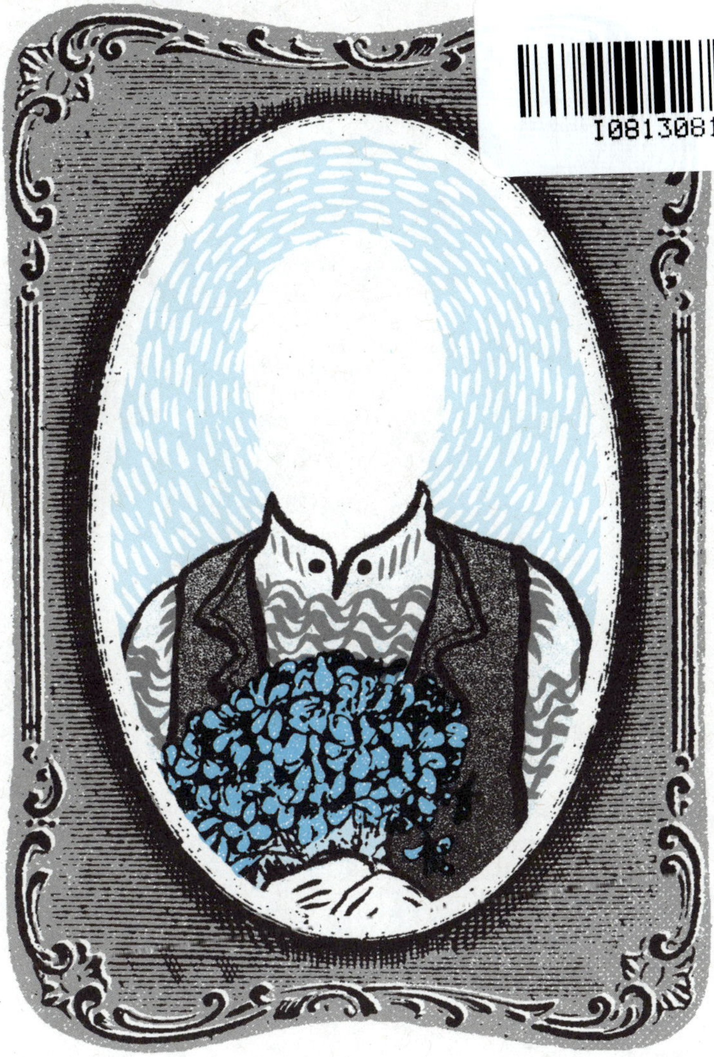

PICTURED ABOVE

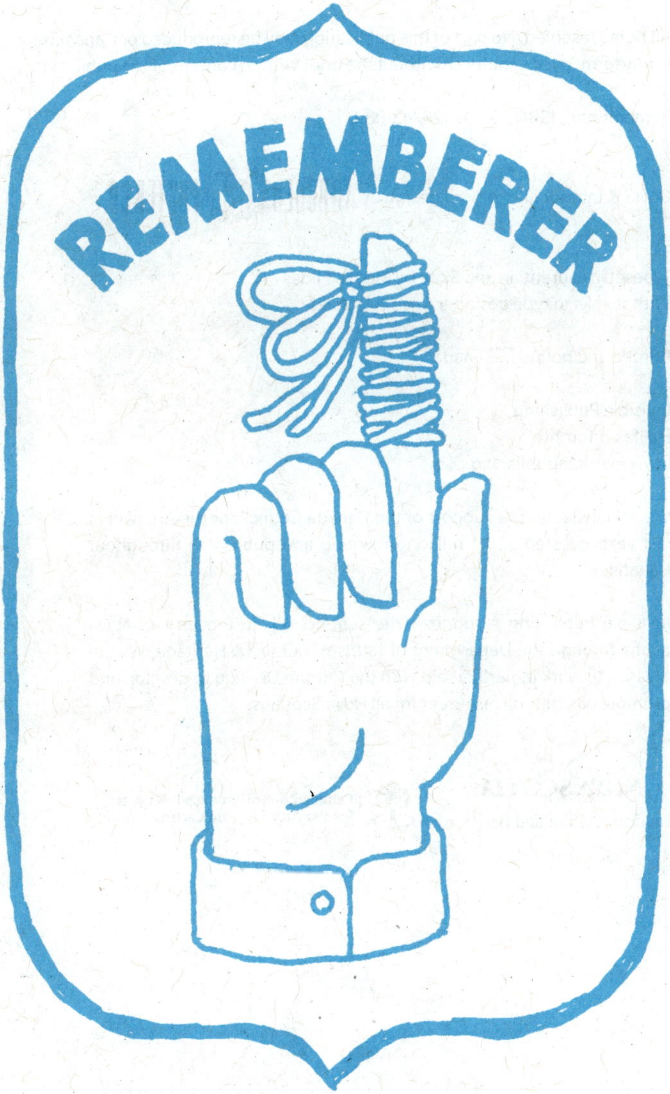
REMEMBERER

Rememberer: ISBN 978-1-926743-08-0

Cover & Interior illustration/design by YORODEO POSTER CO.

Typeset in Laurentian and Slate by Megan Fildes
With thanks to type designer Rod McDonald

Printed and bound in Canada

Invisible Publishing
Halifax & Toronto
www.invisiblepublishing.com

We acknowledge the support of the Canada Council for the Arts which last year invested $20.1 million in writing and publishing throughout Canada.

Invisible Publishing recognizes the support of the Province of Nova Scotia through the Department of Tourism, Culture & Heritage. We are pleased to work in partnership with the Culture Division to develop and promote our cultural resources for all Nova Scotians.

NOVA SCOTIA
Tourism, Culture and Heritage

Canada Council for the Arts
Conseil des Arts du Canada

IMPORTANT INFO

FULL NAME:

DESIRED NAME:

MAILING ADDRESS:

PHONE:	CELL:

EMAIL:

WORK CONTACT:

EYE COLOUR:	BLOOD TYPE:

DOCTOR CONTACT:

EMERGENCY CONTACT:

BIRTHDAY:

ASTROLOGICAL SIGN(S):

RIGHT OR LEFT HANDED:	SKILLS:

FAVOURITE FOOD:

ALLERGIES:	MEDICATION:

PETS:

GREATEST WEAKNESS:

DREAM JOURNAL

JENNER-BROOKE BERGER, *EDITOR*

Everyday You're a Genius

I KNOW THERE'S THE FORGETTING. Searching for the change purse with a whole thirteen dollars in it. Enough money for popsicles from the corner store, enough to keep you cool in this humidity forever.

Dislodged thoughts floating through the frontal, parietal, cortical and unstoppable lobes of your brain.

Losing the birthdays and the phone numbers and the mailing addresses of all the best people you've ever known, and then there's not even finding enough places to store the guilt of it all.

Trouble falling asleep on Sunday nights.

Rushing home to realize you missed the long distance call from the place you can't spell and can't find in the atlas.

Getting lost driving to the beach, finally arriving as the sun goes down and the biggest worst deer flies swarm out from the seaweed. The knowing, the regretting; it's too late to swim.

Clawing for an understanding of why anyone and everyone has left you to your own devices.

Longing for a day, where there's no kind of lonelinesses, not a one. Especially not the kind that blinds you and forces the choices you're not so sure were the right ones.

There are days when you're so far away you can't find yourself inside all the places you'd usually be and it's all so sad and so beautiful you can't help but sit on the steps of someone you don't know and cry. And it hurts to be there, on the steps, but it's also right because it's important and cathartic and where would you be, if not here, empathizing so much it hurts like this, having the terrible ability to feel so much you lose track and without that, would be lesser.

But today I am there with you and we are walking on a quiet street and I trust you because although we perform the terrible sin of feeling sorry for ourselves sometimes, I always know we have this thing in common, that we will never give up on each other.

And then there's finding the time.

Uncovering an entire extra hour due to a daylight saviour that every clock forgot.

Untangling the chords of errands, deadlines, appointments. Being left with perfect straight lines, smoothed out, and away from each other.

Solving the hardest problem of the day, figuring out how to arrange as many people as possible in the back of the van and then riding it all the way to the Ocean.

Dreaming about the person you love, and finding well, shit, they love you too.

Filling the crossword. Finishing the 3D puzzle. Fixing your own bike, car, surf board, guitar, barbecue. The right place at the right time. Luck, speed, agility, warmth, fulfillment, amelioration, the right song, the day break, the sun set, rib-shaking laughter, results, warranted dignity, your own beautiful body and its worth. Losing it all. Finding it right where you left it. Understanding it was there all along.

Remembering.

DOODLER

MONTH OF ______

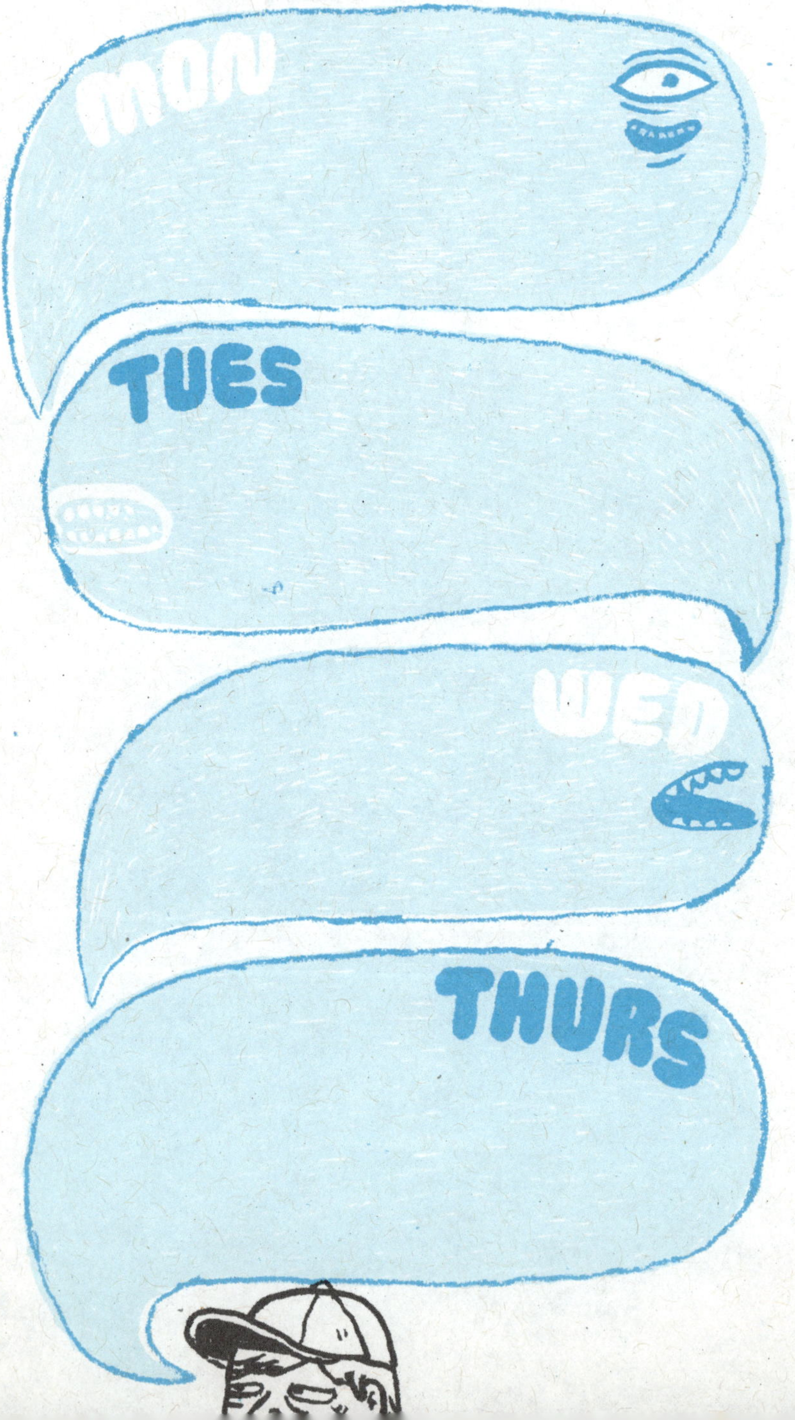

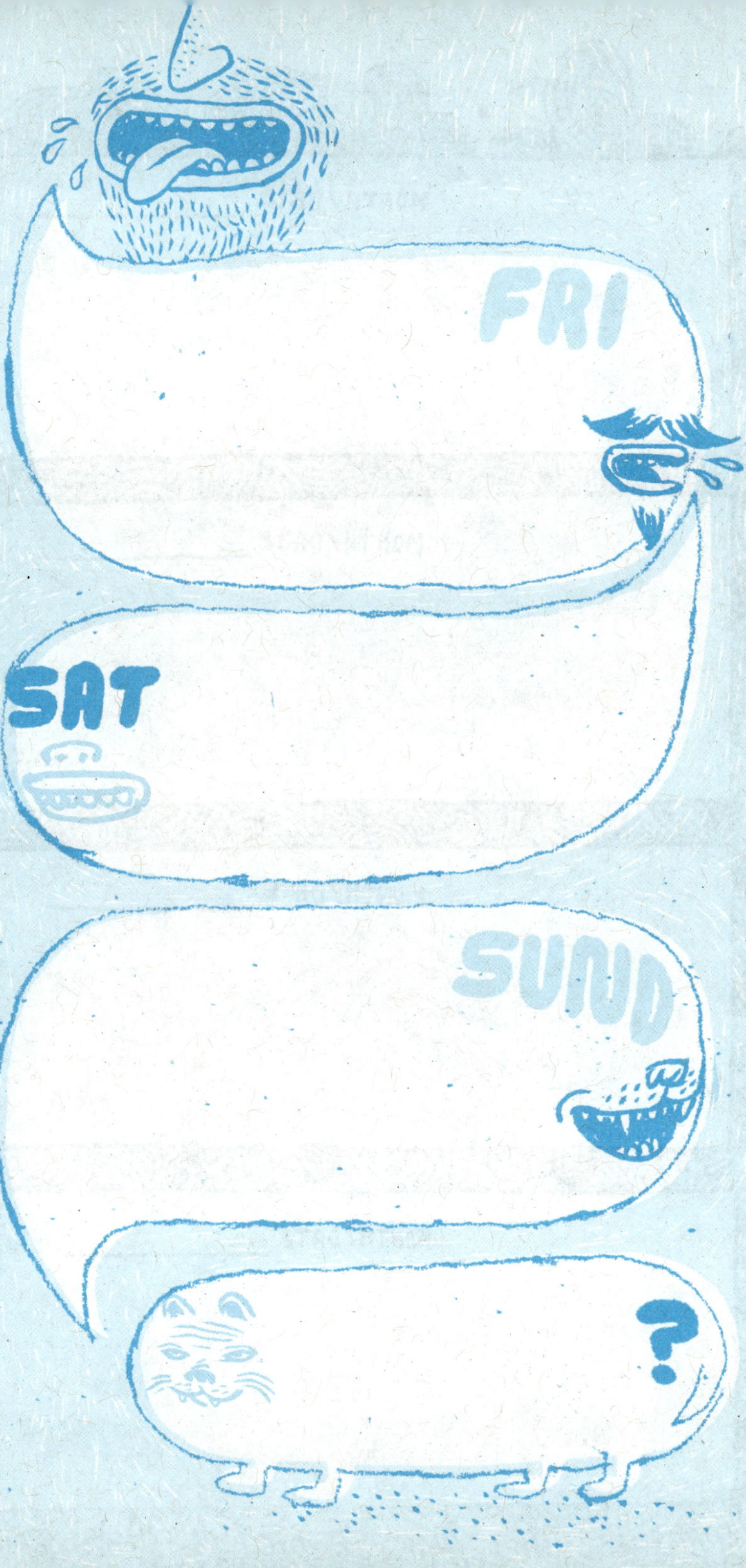
FRI
SAT
SUND
?

MONTH/DATE ______________

MONTH/DATE ______________

MONTH/DATE ______________

MONTH/DATE ______________

MONTH/DATE ______________

MONTH/DATE ______________

MONTH/DATE ______________

MONTH/DATE ______________

IMPORTANT NOTE

BEN STEPHENSON

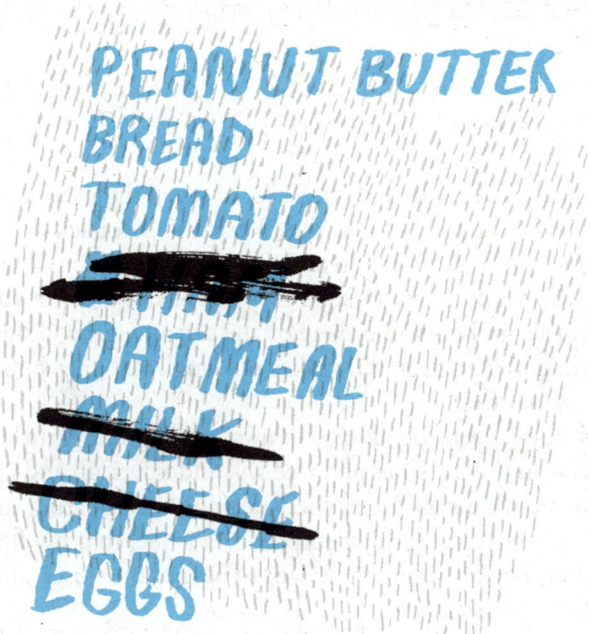

Plantain Supernova

THESE DAYS WHEN I LOOK AT YOU—with the most honest of eyes and without the need to look at myself anymore—I shrink a foot and a half. I am eight years old. I am sitting on the curb in front of my friend's house, and I don't know why, but I am terrified.

My friend notices me nervously fidgeting, squeezing the skin of my left elbow with my right hand. He gets off his bike, stepping off behind the seat, the red bike continues on its own, a ghost bike, sailing, weaving, crashing and melting into a steel heap of itself.

"What's wrong?" he asks me but I can't come up with an answer; I am fifteen years and eighteen inches too short to understand.

"Your bike looks dead," I say.

I don't get out of bed. I write a list of seven things to do on the back of my hand and then I put the pen back on the night table and I don't do one of them. Lying there, I look out the window and it's solid grey like always so I put your face way up there somewhere by the sun and feel you shine warm and it's silly and it makes me laugh just once before it makes me cry.

While I sleep the afternoon away, all clothing articles I own gain unique souls and free will and hover up and join into a whirling cyclone, then decide, after floating and flying over my dreaming corpse for a while, that my floor and my bed are where they want to be, not the closet, and I wake up buried alive.

I finally take a deep breath and pull a red sweater from the heap and go to the store and I am not eight, no, in this sweater I'm sixty-eight, feeling old and perfect. My shiny shoes are shining and inside the door the shopping cart boy notices. "Nice shoes, sir."

I grin and check the second list on my hand:

<u>GET</u>

– peanut butter
– bread
– tomato
– ham
– oatmeal
– milk
– cheese
– eggs

I have collected almost everything I need in my cart, and then I see the tall box of plantains.

"What the heck is a plantain anyway?" I say out loud and no one answers.

While surveying the strange fruits, there is a fracture in the continuum and I suddenly and overwhelmingly remember what it feels like inside my chest when I can make you smile. My chest remembers.

"I think it's some type of potato-banana," I say to me.

"Why not?" I ask my caution as it flies toward the wind—where I have thrown it—and I decide to buy the weird thing.

I use it as a phone, on my way to the cash, and I tell them to cancel the meeting, to cancel everything, to pencil me in later. I tell them they are fired.

The plantain is still at my ear when I see you.

You are in line at the cash and you are hugging me before I register that it's really you.

"I'm sorry," you say.

"Me too."

"I'm so sorry."

"We are sixty-eight now."

"I know. I love you."

"It's too late," I say.

I look around.

"I'm going to have to call you back," I whisper into the plantain and my left arm is numb.

"My arm," I say, and you release me. I see your round face and blue glowing eyes with their inner ring of yellow sparks. I am eight again, I am even less, my age is subtracting years per second, I am falling backwards, smashing into my shopping cart and you want to catch me but you're failing and the cart is blasting off into a display of frying pans, knocking them over, clanging, full of violence.

I am on my back, holding my numb left arm with my right hand and that means that I am finally having a heart attack, and even if it hadn't fallen and bounced so far from me, I wouldn't know how to dial 9-1-1 on the plantain and how tiny it looks now, how tiny it all looks, every single moment was tiny except for this one.

I am crossing things off the lists in my mind. I got every grocery, I even got an extra; It was a good day. But there are other lists, so many of them, but maybe they are shrinking. You are kneeling over me and your face is in shock, it is distant and open, miles away, a ghost.

"I love you too," I say, "I have always loved you since the first moment, since before that, I will–"

"Call an ambulance!" you scream to everyone, and the sounds all start to fade and I keep looking at you and I am captivated. You smile after such a long time, after I smile long enough to make you. "It's OK," I say, and you are shaking.

"I've never had anyone be so patient with me," you say, with your hand on my red sweatery chest.

"It's OK," I say. In the tininess I have nothing to be afraid of and people probably think we're weird, have always thought we were weird at every step of our weird way, but especially right now, on the floor and everything, with the plantain. I look at you and notice again how you were crafted so expertly. I see how you smile with every muscle in your body. I see how you have a brightness you wear on the inside. The supermarket is made of prisms and light, and I am exploding in on myself. "Maybe patient and weird were all I ever wanted to be," I say.

You light up and laugh and my heart does something foreign and vaguely painful and I'm eight. Less. I am dimming to three, two, one, I am nothing.

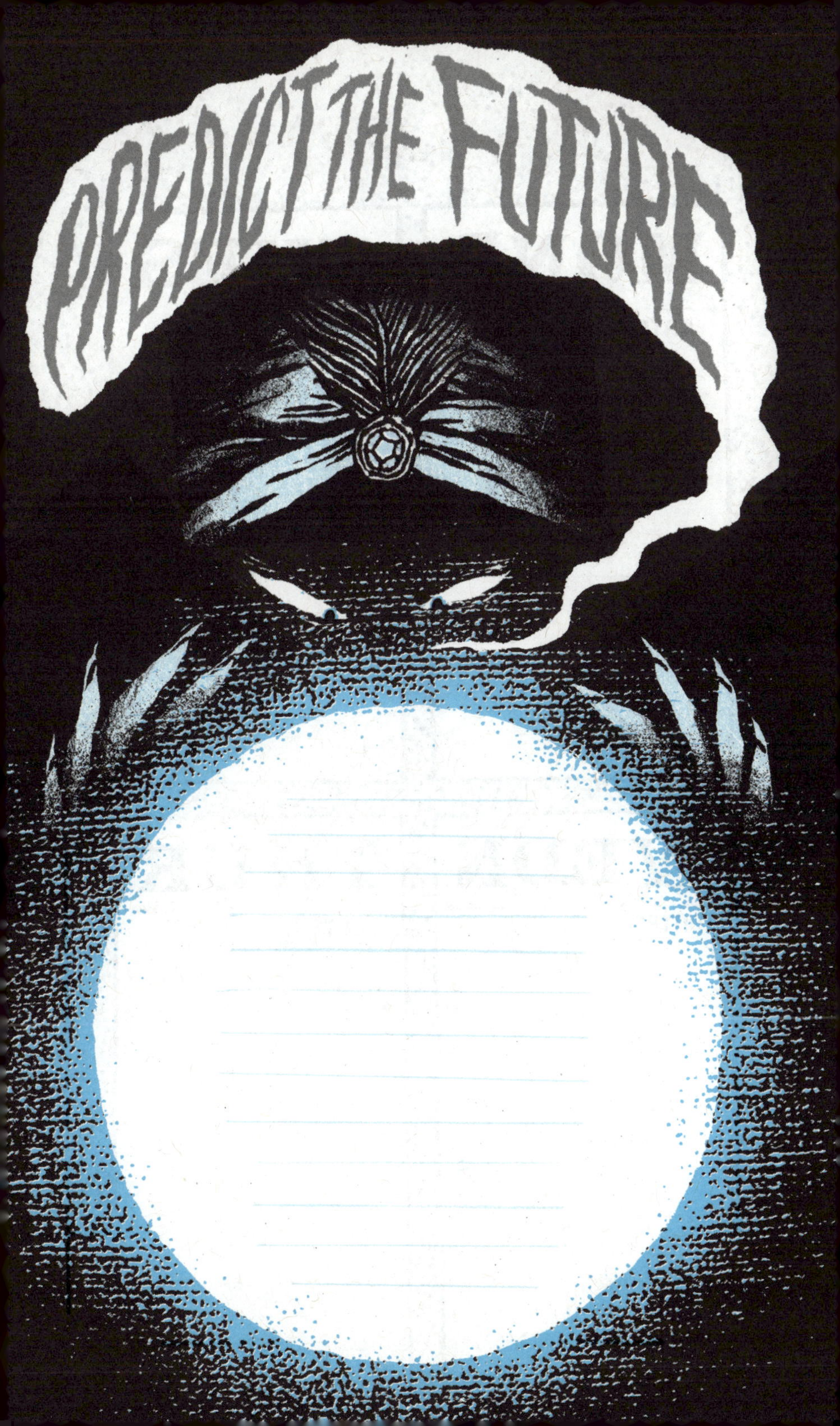
PREDICT THE FUTURE

MOND

DATE:

TUES

DATE:

WEDN

DATE:

THUR

DATE:

FRID

DATE:

SATU

DATE:

SUND

DATE:

&

MON

MONTH:

DATE:

TUES

MONTH:

DATE:

WED

MONTH:

DATE:

THUR

MONTH:

DATE:

FRI

MONTH: DATE:

SAT

MONTH: DATE:

SUN

MONTH: DATE:

ETC

WHATEVER:

A MONTH CALLED

MONDAY DATE

TUESDAY DATE

WEDNESDAY DATE

THURSDAY DATE

FRIDAY DATE

SATURDAY DATE

SUNDAY DATE

EXTRA

MONTH:

MON

TUES

WED

THUR

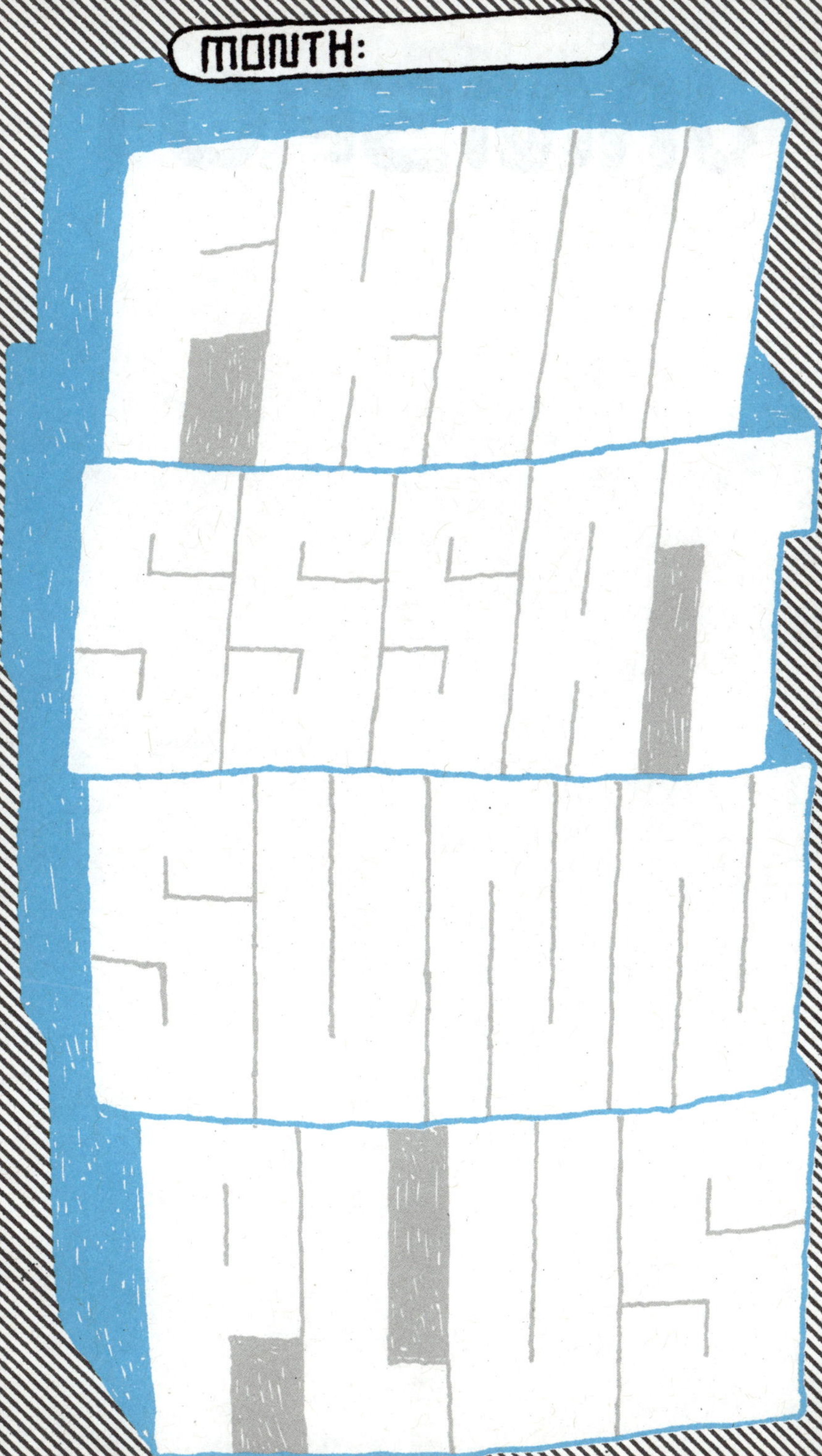
MONTH:

JAMSPOT

LAURA DAWE

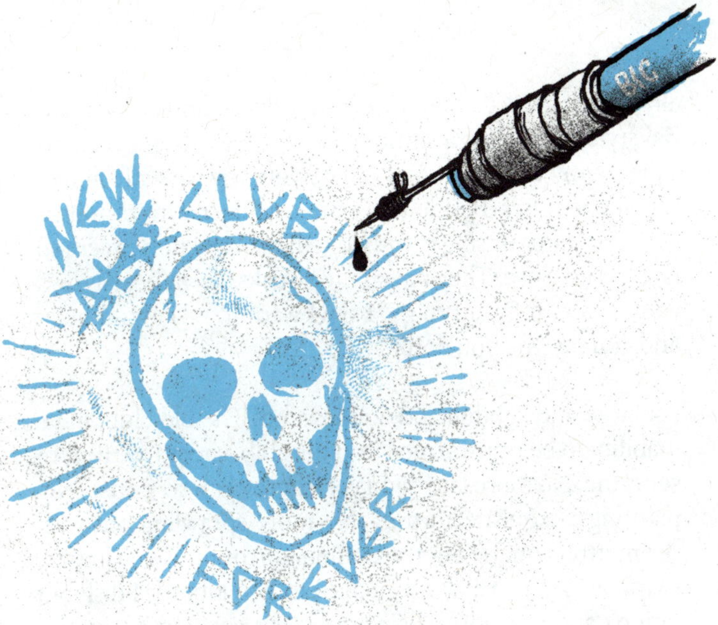

Green Grasser

Woody Allen never wanted to be part of any club that would have him as a member.

I applied to you for years and years and years. When I was finally accepted I tread light and in awe, but when I was nominated president the whole thing became gauche and unappealing. The drugged out, rock n roll four a.m., parties that your establishment is known for lack glamour from the inside. I find myself on the deck in black leather boots, high as a kite, swaying, staring across the river to a quiet, moon-lit gala. The simple gowns glitter and occasionally I catch a word about incorporation, so-and-so's directorial style, saving for a summer home. You stagger out and squeeze my ass and I turn to kiss you, my ears still aimed across the water. Beside us a famous singer with tattoos is fucking a famous singer with long hair. They don't seem so famous up close. They haven't for weeks. I sigh heavily and you ask soft if I want to go. I say I want to talk about taxes and you say "no you don't."

I subdue and subdue and condescend. The old club, in its inability to be transformed into the club across the river, resents me. No more late nights of improv jam sessions, drug paintings, exquisite corpses. No more sprawling out with the mattress on the floor, watching horror movies. They try to follow my lead around a table-clothed table as I dish out quinoa and avocado. Their tattoos are covered by neutral tones tailored by up-and-coming local designers. We are all unhappy.

They are sad when I leave them because I have played the trick that works best when it comes to winning admirers: make them feel like less.

I cross the water in stealthy boat, relieved I only gave myself one tattoo.

I have made it to the fancy club at last. This is where I belong. I charm my way in at the door and slip into many conversations. For weeks I try to win over the women. They are so beautiful and tall. The men and I talk work and art and money. I am often excluded but hell, isn't that what I wanted? The club is colder than I expected, emptier. The women often stand on the deck looking across the river to where loud laughter and heavy music blares. They sip white wine and when they get too drunk they fight with their husbands and cry in the bathroom. I get realdrunk one night and crazydance. I blast the music and squig all over the floor. My fucking stupid dress rips and I laugh and rip it more. Everyone tries to join in but they can only dance, not freak out. Furious now, I smash a crystal vase on the floor. I can't stop crying until I look up to their horrored faces and then I laugh and laugh. I jump off the deck into the river.

I want to swim back to you but it's really far.

WEEK OF EVENTS

MON MONTH DATE

TUE MONTH DATE

WED MONTH DATE

THU MONTH DATE

FRI MONTH DATE

SAT MONTH DATE

SUN MONTH DATE

LUNDI

DATE:

MARDI

DATE:

MERCREDI

DATE:

JEUDI

DATE:

VENDREDI

DATE:

SAMEDI

DATE:

DIMANCHE

DATE:

DEMAIN

DATE:

MONDAY DATE:

TUESDAY DATE:

WEDNESDAY DATE:

THURSDAY DATE:

FRIDAY DATE:

SATURDAY DATE:

SUNDAY DATE:

NOTES

LITTLE LISTS

TERI VLASSOPOULOS

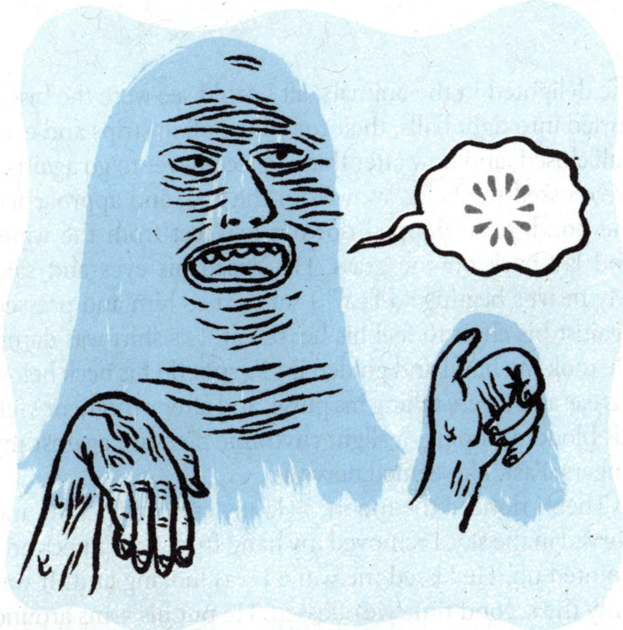

Seeing Things

KAREN SEES THE GHOST

First there were the peacocks. We were in the park and it was late and we heard shrieks, like children getting their fingernails ripped off or worse. Jesse looked at me and his eyes were huge, terrified. We took off running and maybe we were screaming too. When we remembered we were near the zoo we stopped, walked back, and the birds were still shrieking, stupid and loud, and we laughed at ourselves. The zoo is small, a random collection of the saddest looking animals: goats, bison, peacocks. I told Jesse about the last time I visited. I went with my 7 year old cousin and while she delighted in the animals, all I could see were the bison curled into tight balls, their fur falling off in strips and eyes half closed, and how after that I vowed never to go again. We crossed the field, away from the zoo, and approached the pond. Jesse flopped down a few feet from the water and lay back on the grass. He closed his eyes and said, "My heart's beating so fast." I sat next to him and pressed against his chest to feel his heartbeat. His shirt was damp. He took my hand and guided it to a spot on his neck below his ear as if I were taking his pulse, and after a moment I felt his blood pumping, a slight rhythmic pressure against my fingers. Fast. He seemed nervous.

Then I noticed the moon, a skinny crescent, yellow and curved in the sky. I removed my hand from Jesse's neck and pointed up. He kissed me while I was looking at it. It was only the second time we'd kissed. He put his arms around me and we were on the ground again. If the peacocks were still shrieking I didn't hear them. For awhile everything seemed quiet, not just the park, but the universe too. Everything concentrated into us, the only two points of heat on that cool summer night. It was after midnight and no one knew we were there. My parents thought I was at home in bed.

Afterwards I got up to brush the dirt off my clothes and out of my hair, and the skin on the back of my thighs was indented from the blades of grass beneath me. Jesse was still on the ground and he reached up to run his fingers over them. I sat back down and for the next fifteen minutes we hardly talked, but it wasn't strange, the quiet, it was comfortable.

Finally there was the ghost. I saw him first. Jesse was looking up, not straight ahead. The ghost was standing in the pond, the water up to his shins, and he was staring at us, and I thought of the peacocks and how I'd run away so quickly from them, how instinctive it was. This time I didn't run. "Look," I said to Jesse.

We stared back at him. He flickered.

JESSE SEES THE GHOST

When we see the ghost Karen leans towards it and I lean back. It vanishes so quickly that when it's gone we don't know what to do. Karen's eyes are bright and her cheeks are flushed, and I'm not sure if it's because we just had sex or just saw a ghost, but she's glowing.

I've seen this ghost before, a year ago, only for a split second, and I was drunk, so the next day I didn't know if I'd hallucinated it or not. What proof did I have that it was real? I was walking through the park on my way home after a party. I'd turned seventeen three days earlier and my grandfather had just died, and everything was confusing. I hadn't even met Karen yet; I didn't know she existed. I wanted to sit by the pond and get my thoughts straightened out. The ghost was in a tree close to the water, its legs dangling over a branch. His or its? If ghosts have gender, this one was male. It took me a few minutes to realize he was there. First I thought it was my grandfather, but it didn't look like him. It wasn't old enough. The ghost opened its mouth to say something, but before any sound came out I got up and bolted. When I got to the edge of the park, I threw up, and then I went home and slept for 14 hours straight. How could it have been real, I asked myself.

I didn't tell anyone about the ghost, but I'd bring people to the same spot hoping they'd see it too. Nothing strange ever happened. I met Karen a few months later, and brought her to the park. I'd only go late at night and I was surprised when she agreed to come with me. I was so surprised that for a while I forgot I was looking for the ghost.

That night the sky was dark, but there was a moon. It was darker while we were walking, when we were surrounded in trees and couldn't see the sky. But the darkest thing was the pond. I looked at the water and it was black. I closed my eyes but it wasn't the same kind of darkness. It wasn't real, if real means that I can show it to someone else. The ghost was transparent, like water when it's not black, when it's not late at night. The ghost couldn't have been real either, I don't think, but if Karen saw him too, that's something.

THE GHOST SEES KAREN AND JESSE

I had a dream when I was twelve years old, and I remembered it for the rest of my life, and I remember it still. It was a prophecy, maybe, or advice.

In the dream I'm alone, and it's night and I'm walking beside a railroad track. The track stretches on forever, and it snakes through a large, dark field. In the distance there are towns glowing with orange light. I'm between towns, but I'm not afraid.

In the dream I don't feel lonely because I'm two entities at once—the person walking and the person watching—and both of us are thinking the same thoughts and both of us are peaceful. We're concentrating on the horizon, the orange lights. They're like fireflies or flames, beckoning. It's tiring walking for so long, but we know that eventually we'll reach them and that when we do we'll rest, sleep, all sweet and warm, so one of us keeps watching and the other one keeps marching, and we keep going and going, following the tracks and nearing those lights.

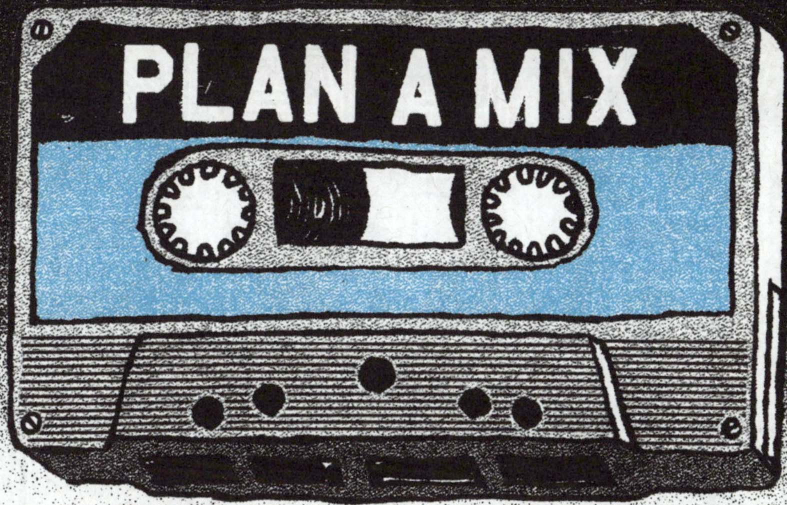

SIDE A

SIDE B

CHOOSE WISELY

WEEK DAZE

MON

MONTH DATE

TUE

MONTH DATE

WED

MONTH DATE

THU

MONTH DATE

FRI

MONTH DATE

SAT

MONTH DATE

SUN

MONTH DATE

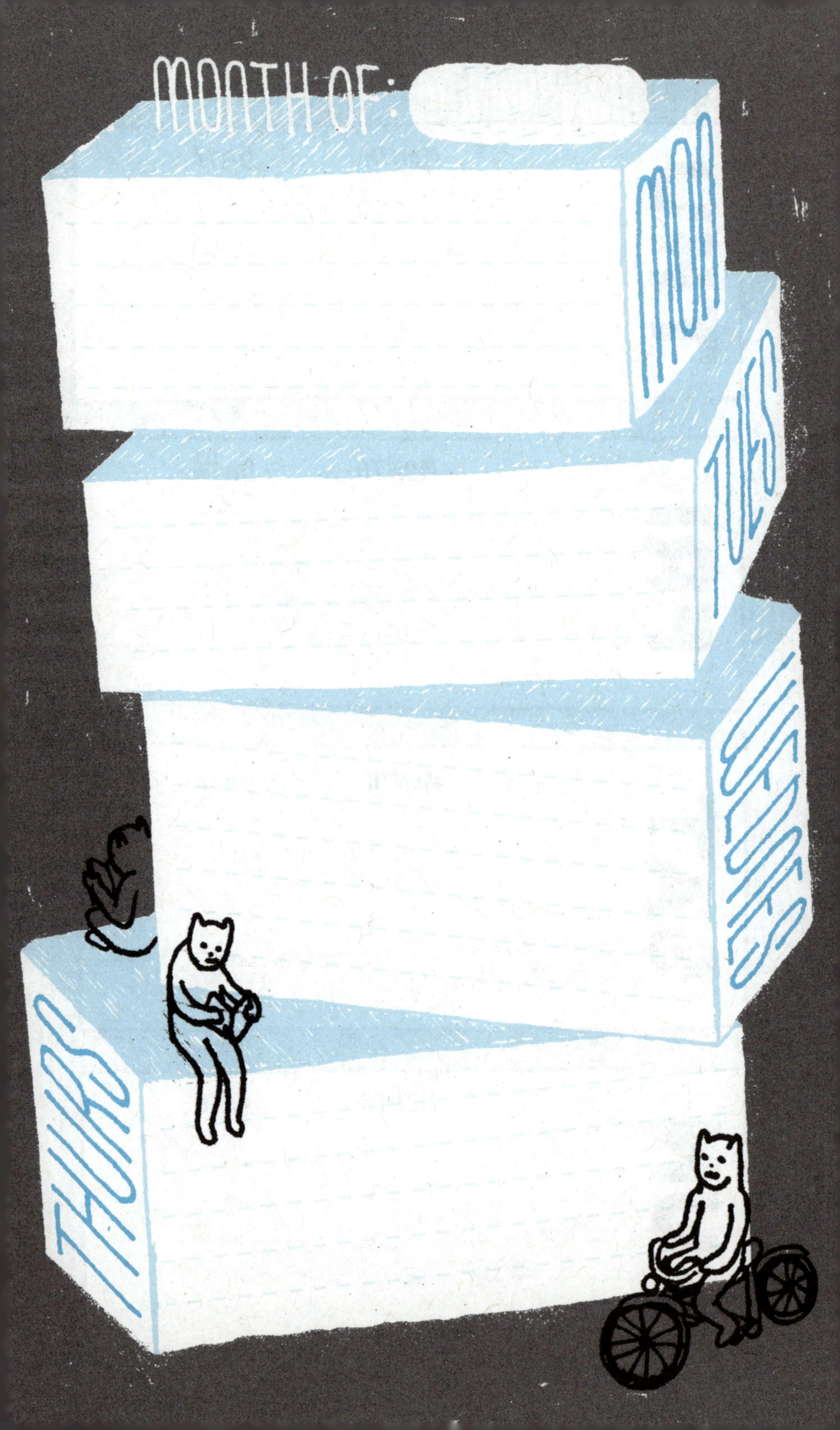
MONTH OF:
MON
TUES
WEDNES
THURS

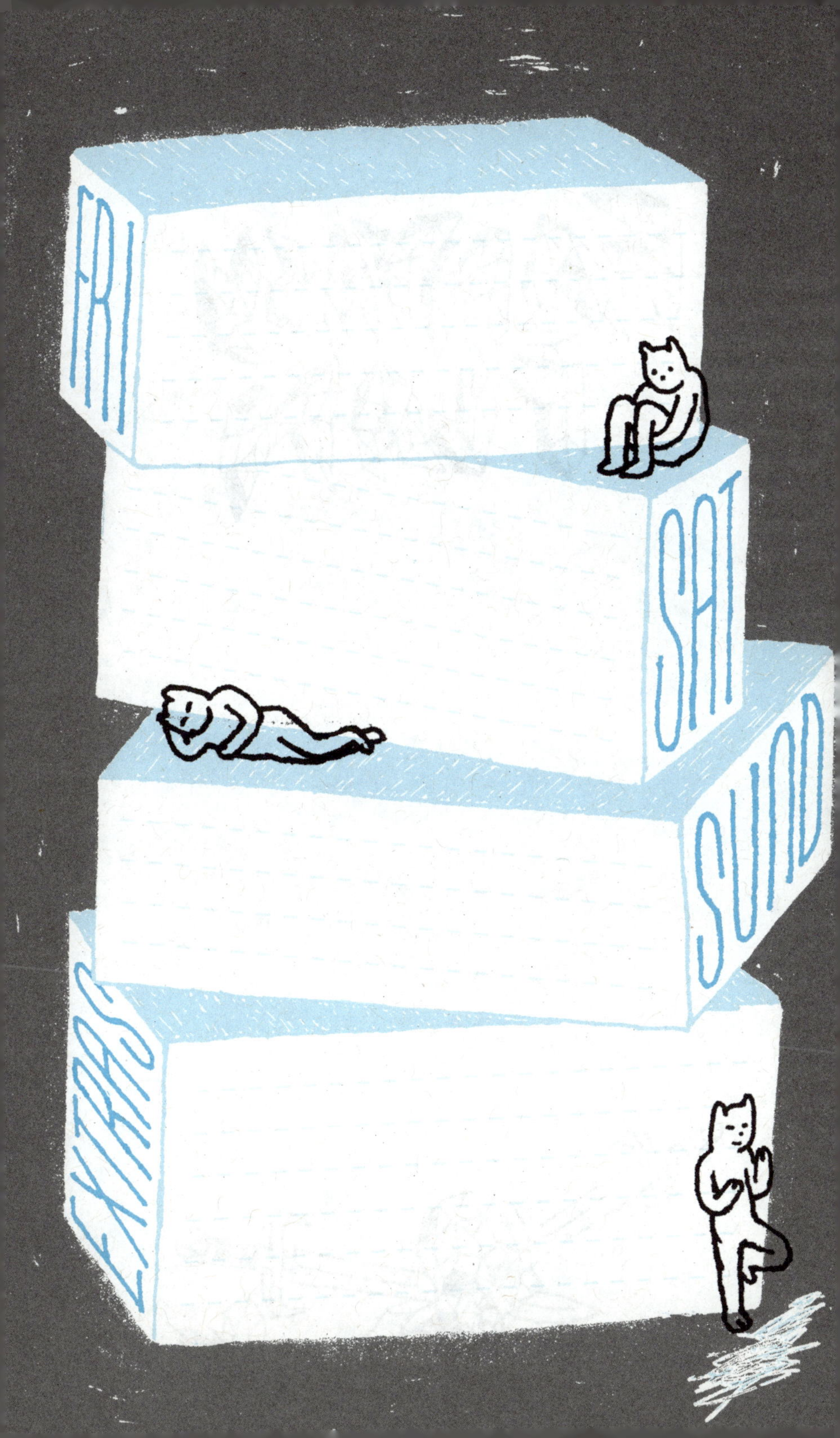
FRI
SAT
SUND
EXTRAS

FANTASY PLAN

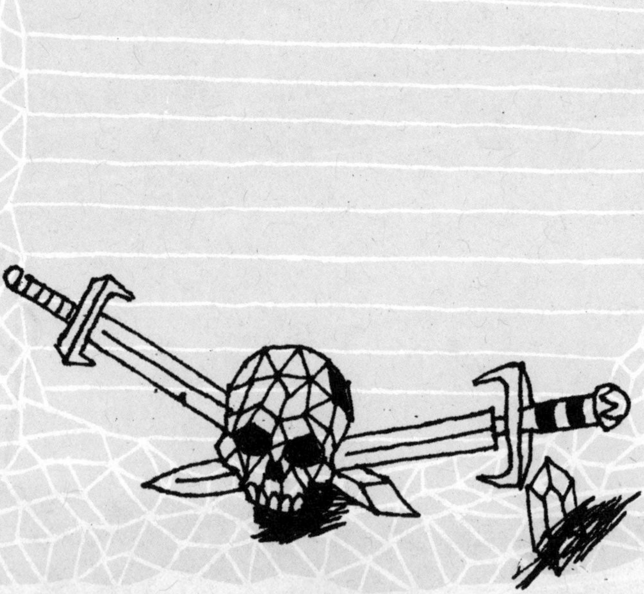

MINDY HUNG

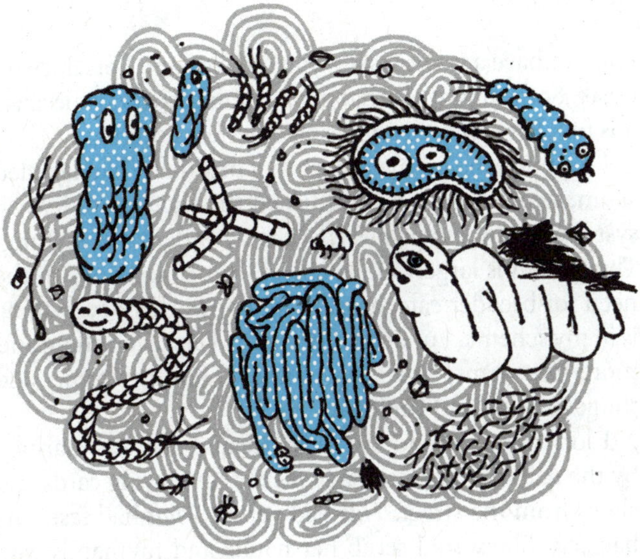

Lost, Found

YESTERDAY, I SAW a teenage girl drop a gum wrapper on the ground. I picked it up and ran after her as she sauntered on. "Miss, excuse me, did you drop this?" I asked. "Miss?"

She looked puzzled, then seeing my hand, her face grew hard. She said, "Hey, you got a problem with me?"

She smacked my upturned palm. It stung.

The paper fluttered to the ground. I watched the girl saunter away. Not knowing what else to do, I picked up the square, smoothed it out, and I brought it home.

I do not have a wastebasket, you see, because I produce no waste. Some might say that my bungalow is untidy because it is full. For some, cleanliness is a perfect nothing.

I dropped the gum wrapper in a box that I had labelled "Gum, Accessories" and I returned the shoebox to its vast system. In my bungalow, there is an order to everything. The system is largely alphabetical with concessions to the need for broader categorization. I know where everything is in my schema. I understand where I keep everything and, more important, why. I have time to knit my brows and think about it, and I enjoy it.

I lost my girlfriend last year because she was alarmed by the fact that I occasionally picked up playing cards and shoes from the street. *This* had germs. *That* had festering bacteria. She would scrub her hands and my hands with alcohol-based sanitizer. She would wash our faces with it. She said it smelled so good, that she would drink it, if she could. But she couldn't so much as stomach a white wine spritzer, oddly enough.

After a while, even when I was coated with disinfectant, she could not bring herself to touch my fingers, much less anything else. I remember begging her to kiss me, begging her to try, one last time. But the sky had begun to darken and she wanted to get home before it rained.

She phoned later and told me she would not come out any more. It would rain again. She would get dirty again. I told her that the sun was out now, and she said that it didn't matter, because the clouds would emerge again at any minute. The sky could pour grey water onto her cheeks and skin, and god knows where all of that liquid had been.

I grew alarmed. I went to her house, her white house on

a short street, and knocked on the door. She didn't answer. But she called to me and told me that she couldn't make herself touch the doorknob. After a while, she stopped being able to speak into the telephone receiver.

I still go by her house, now and then, when I am collecting. Gathering things, picking things up, categorizing--it takes up more of my time now, so I do not always have a chance to stop by her place, to leave a cucumber sandwich with the crusts cut off, or a thermos of soup. Sometimes I see a flicker in the window, a shadow passing. But the grass has grown long and all of her pink petunias have died. I suspect that whoever lives there can't be her. But still, I try to go.

I am sad to abandon someone, or something, anything. For me, organization is about putting pieces together. To discard an item because it no longer seems to fit—it is disorderly.

MOND

DATE:

TUES

DATE:

WEDN

DATE:

THUR

DATE:

FRID

DATE:

SATU

DATE:

SUND

DATE:

&

MONDAY

DATE:

TUESDAY

DATE:

WEDNESDAY

DATE:

THURSDAY

DATE:

FRIDAY

DATE:

SATURDAY

DATE:

SUNDAY

DATE:

NOTES

~~DATE~~:

LUNDI

DATE:

MARDI

DATE:

MERCREDI

DATE:

JEUDI

DATE:

VENDREDI

DATE:

SAMEDI

DATE:

DIMANCHE

DATE:

DEMAIN

DATE:

A DETAILED ACCOUNT OF WHAT HAPPENED

DATE:

GEORDIE MILLER

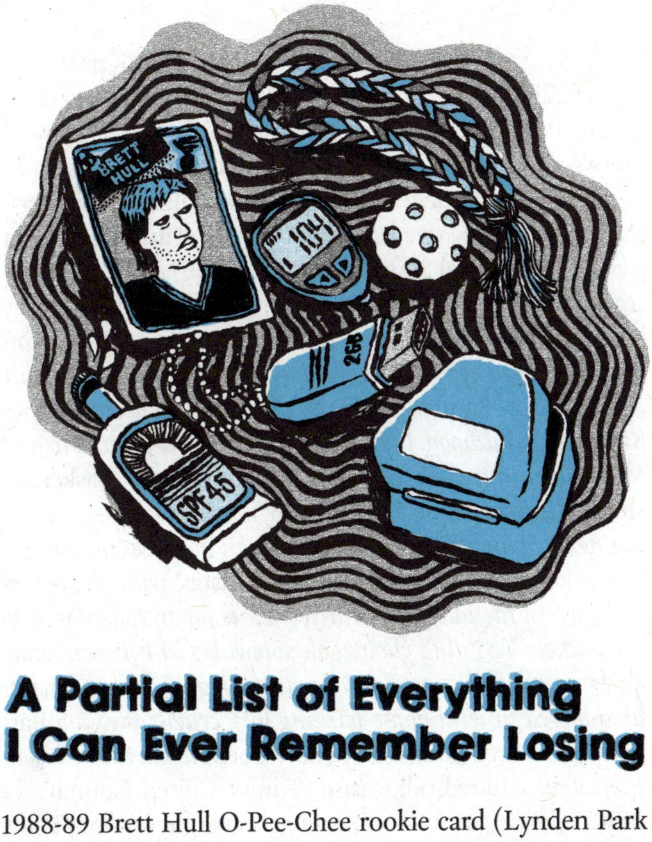

A Partial List of Everything I Can Ever Remember Losing

1988-89 Brett Hull O-Pee-Chee rookie card (Lynden Park Mall) *Impossibly I explore the dirty Branford mall, playing a reel that villainizes all the children's faces, like that 'Runaway Train' video* Mark's power blue Paul Newman sweater (Quinpool Perks) *which could never, I could never, be as funny as you* Glucometer (Car #2214) *spend your life with machines that keep you alive and always forgetting* Snub-nosed .38 cap gun (Aunt Mirney and Uncle Normy's backyard) *Mom's family some mutant race of stale living rooms, I miss* Key to the Kubota (the outfield) *the way the gate would close loudly, like we'd accomplished something together* QLINK password (right brain) *with my phonological loop, words now nowhere, hiding* Powder blue Wrestlemania lunch box (Kirklyn's mom's van) *from you, Kirklyn, when you got older and weirder, I couldn't deal* Whiffle softball (Halifax Commons) *the blow the bat agrees to make* Green Timberland rain jacket (Riley's Pool Snooker & Poker Club) *aimless down a street in, of all places, this suburb of London, tonight* Danny Bear (Triumph Hotel) *you are with me, we turn the van around, you're in the arms of someone at the front desk, waiting.* Christine Squires (maturity) *You didn't. I hear you're in Kitchener, adulthood. I never should have slow-danced to Joni Mitchell in that girl's kitchen.* Nike Air 'Wayup' basketball shoes (Iroquois Ride High School) *Suicides to be avoided, our next opponent so much smaller than the losses to come* Six house keys (cement, grass, ponds, plastic) *with me, across the lawn of the lady who will yell at us for trespassing, into the pockets we didn't choose, on sidewalks in-between home and somewhere else, under car seats with gum, fuzz, heat, bits, abandoned funeral home parking lots, cruelly big, you* Bart Simpson skateboard (Burgoyne Woods) *think the hill is an invitation* Quilted pillowcase (Trinity United Church) *for mischief. A boy with the same name as me put his head down for the night and never picked it up again. Our Vice-Principal slowly over the intercom, stopping us up. If we act like we knew him, maybe we did. Mrs. McLeod tried to teach us Hamlet, but those lines didn't stand a chance. We died through him, then went on* red whale-watching hat (Atlantic Ocean) *not seeing what we came for, but* Friendship bracelet from Kelly and Alicia (Lincoln Theatre) *if you ask me once more, I won't let my insecurities wander into our phone conversation dressed as rejection. No, I won't say "no," why* Counting Crows/Wallflowers ticket stub (Wendy's) *order a large Frosty, they're too hard to finish* iPod alarm clock (badlands) *with delicacy, the crime committed* Christmas Tree stand (Robie St. closet) *was our first. A closet somewhere preserves* Canadian passport (Kingston) *these selves I wasn't: the Pizza King of an a.m. court on Princess St., feckless hallway hormone monitor, freckled yes-man to all authority, MSN confessor, lead singer to every band that never existed, silent partner in atrocity, limbo participant, gifted, drunk driver, hunchback. Now we can see that* Protruding ears (Otoplasty) *science sanctions the obvious* Blue retainer case (Leonard Hall) *like how we wouldn't face that monster* Monogrammed flask (my sister's apartment) *e.e. cummings, who said too much, which was not enough, for us* VISA card (Ithaca, NY) *to hope our gas tanks are full of destinations. If walking won't wash the oil off* Kate's 'Stop Making Sense' DVD (Organ Bar) *dance until you're a preposition, between* Bag of sea glass (Avondale Dairy Bar) *the sand, such treasures. Opposition under the sun, reflected in the panting bodies of the beach volleyball game, our texture versus colour debate, "hamburger or hotdog, boys?" looming* 27 bars of soap (drains, residue) *over my head I store my gaze so as not to incur stranger crotches, everywhere* 'Murder in Little Egypt' by Darcy O'Brien (Camp Pinecrest) *homesick for anywhere. A long letter detailing all the dear things now exchangeable for liberation, including allowances, siblings, and baseball gloves. At camp brush teeth in the lake at dark the counselors so mean wet the bed a book about a man who killed his family invented allergies campfire sweater early morning J-stroke almost ran away* 173 golf balls (rivers, woods, private property, fescue, dusk) *come back nines and frontlines, boundaries because* Eric's colourful plaid longsleeve shirt (Gus' Pub) *the stage-side faction wore permanent disguises, were thieves without trying to* Goblin King Magic card (Oakridge Public School climbers) *fail all you fallen playground pebbles, spread into shouts that depart with the bell, remain* Chris Webber Golden State Warriors jersey (Copenhagen) *indifferent mouthfuls of words in an unfamiliar language. Each subway stop a vocabulary exercise, the bad student refuses to consult the directions to, where exactly* SPF-45 suntan lotion (Wet 'n' Wild) *do we take these small claims, courting stiff necks, amnesia, alcoholism, malpractice, arthritis from bumper cars, Ferris Wheel, Tilt-a-Whirls, skeet ball, log flumes? I apprenticed in fraud at the carnival, the son of a lawyer who was also the son of a lawyer, amused* Nana's copy of her father's unpublished novel about World War I (house fire) *when the furnace blew up, my younger brother watched from our neighbour's lawn, laughing as our house kept the fire entertained. A different trauma bound under my bed, smoke bookmarking the pages, ash and embers. The closest we got* Key to Tim and Michelle's cottage (Lake Erie) *was the edge of the water, smooth, sociopath, we waited for a still to show the fluorescent macaroni scarf. Never. So broke-and-entered the air-conditioner window, into a humid evening and a cabin of stars to drink our beers inside, calm* 'Ironman' watch (Algonquin Park) *bears emerge in the midnight of our suburban wilderness adventure. Fear made me honestly believe that the airplane above us was not an airplane above us but a Black Bear. You peed on your leg, retreating at my false alarm, through the tent door, later giggling ourselves to sleep when the next plane invalidates my story* Three paragraphs of 'Suder'-Lacan (non-undeletable Hard Drive space) *essay full of misrecognitions and incoherent desires* 'Grave Dancers' Union' by Soul Asylum (Lisa MacDonald's parent's basement) *at recess, talk of the party speculates on what fates the spun bottle will align, on whether the third track constitutes a good slow song, not to mention that if Leah likes Johnny and Johnny likes Stacey and Stacey likes Mike and Mike likes calling unknown adults and adopting identities that make Tim, especially, crack up, where does it end* USB stick (MapleBear staff room) *in tangled knots, time, can you, stroll after dinner surrounded by the curious procession, people discovering their legs alongside secrets in this new latitude, absurd* Loose change (upholstery, plaster, the economy, sand, dirt) *lost economies amount to more and more walls, the architecture of your lies, of this sentence, well-worn* Family Studies duo-tang (Sir Winston Churchill Secondary School cafeteria) *facts: he won't come back; we got busy growing up, getting jobs—stop me because you've heard this one. He never woke up; we never stop telling, selecting a single moment to cover the rest, going on* Michael Jordan cartoon-head t-shirt (Glenridge Public School boys' locker room) *impossibly.*

MONDAY DATE:

TUESDAY DATE:

WEDNESDAY DATE:

THURSDAY DATE:

FRIDAY

DATE:

SATURDAY

DATE:

SUNDAY

DATE:

NOTES

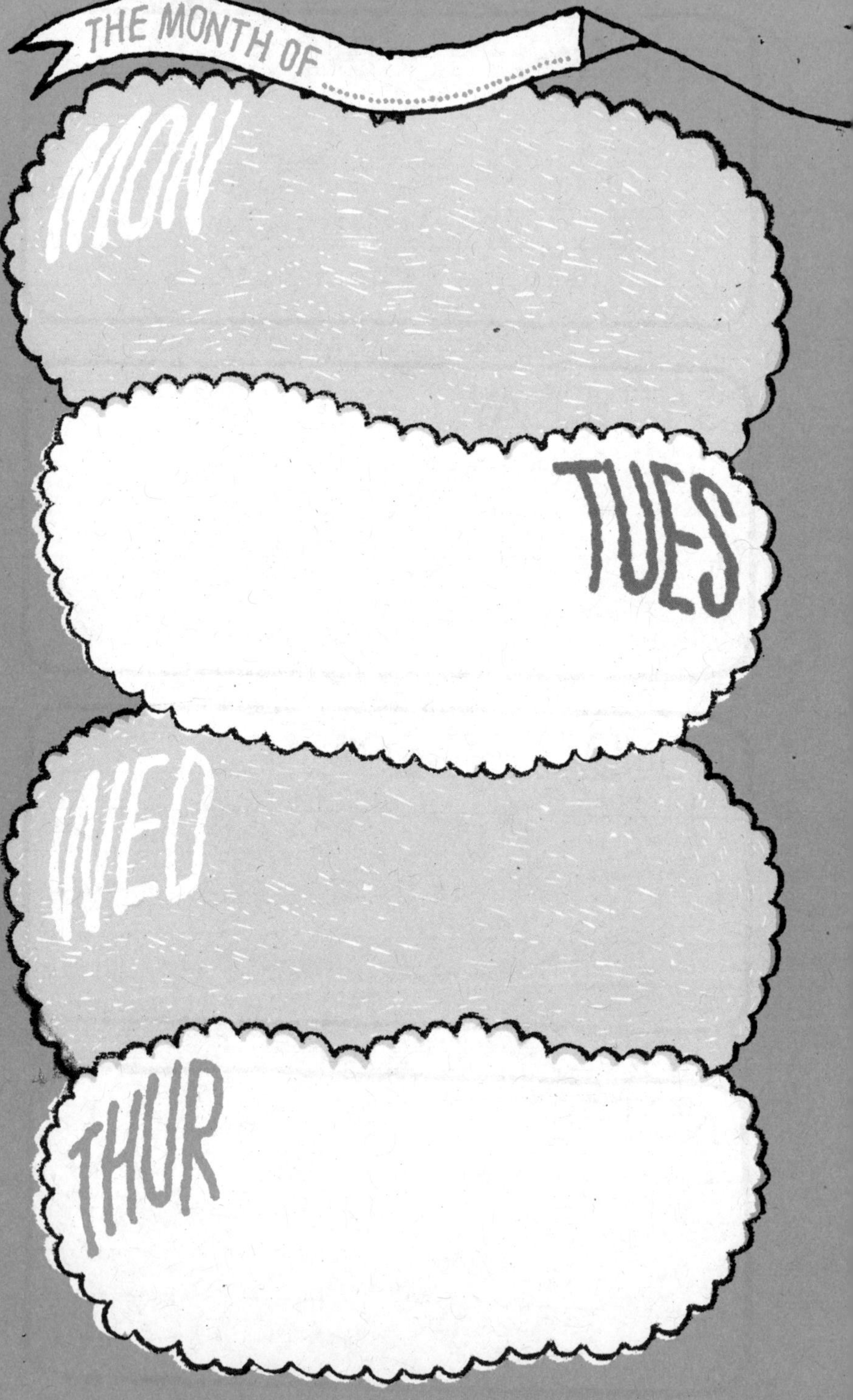

THE MONTH OF
MON
TUES
WED
THUR

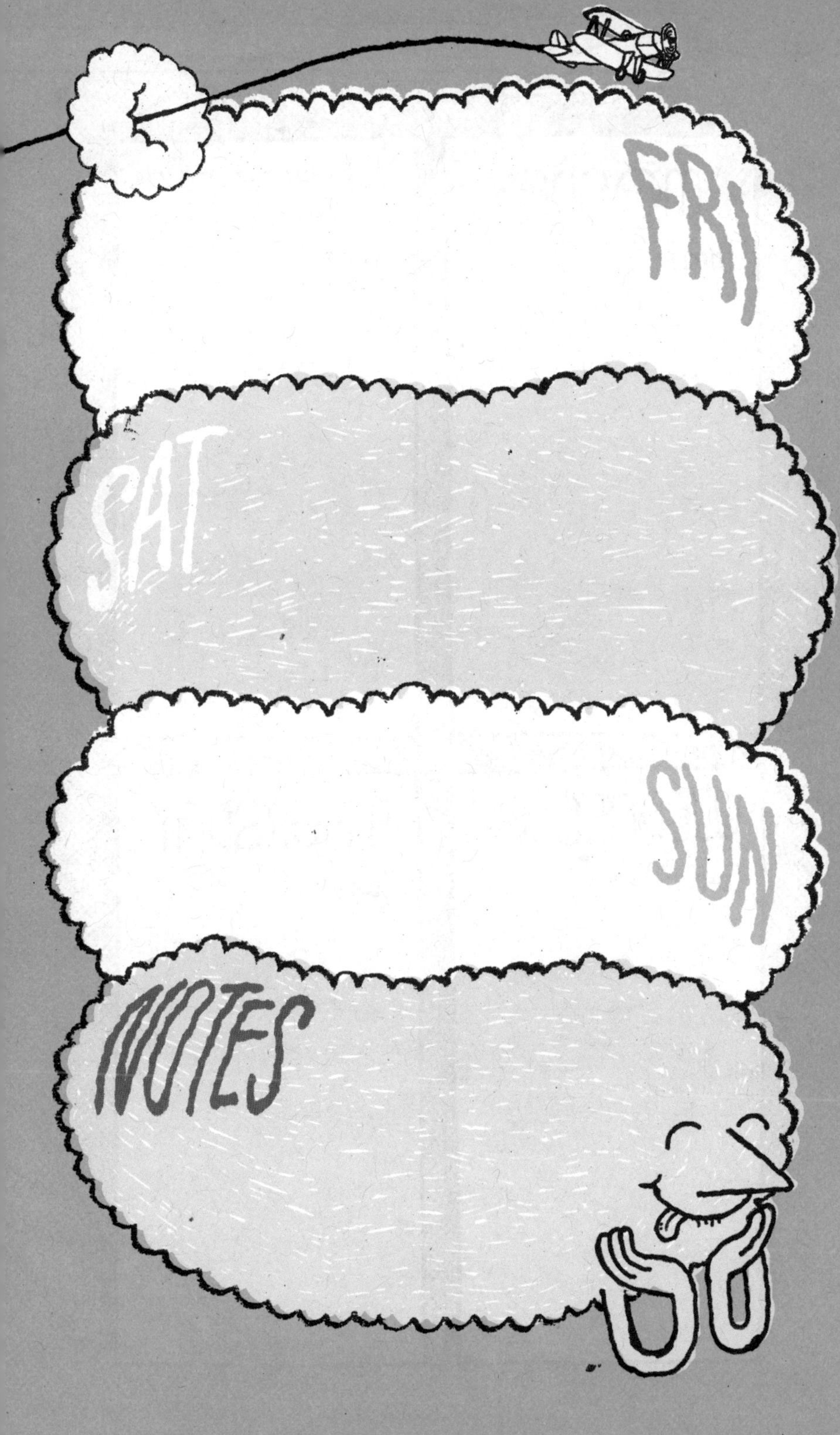
FRI
SAT
SUN
NOTES

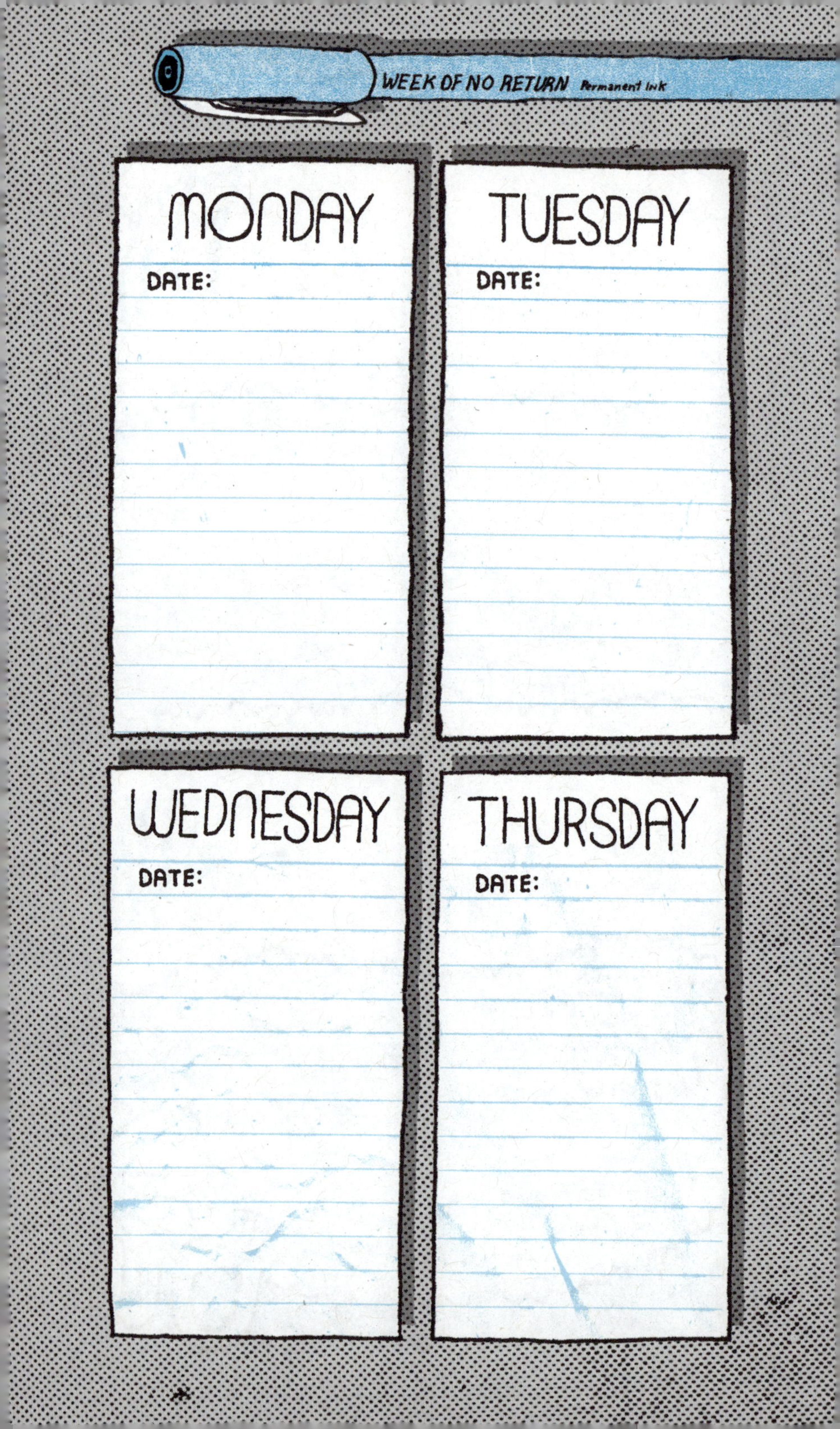
WEEK OF NO RETURN Permanent ink
MONDAY
DATE:
TUESDAY
DATE:
WEDNESDAY
DATE:
THURSDAY
DATE:

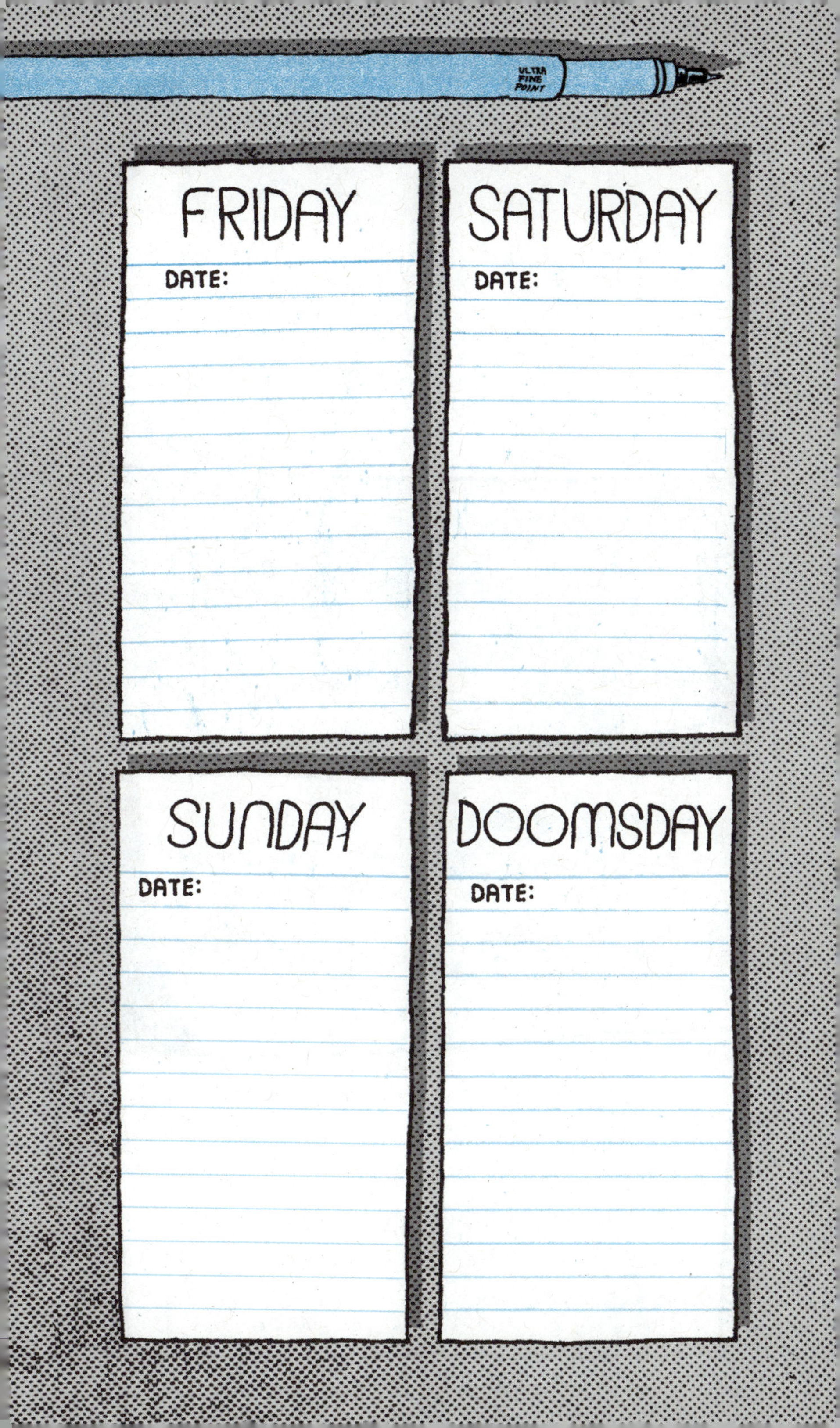
ULTRA FINE POINT
FRIDAY
DATE:
SATURDAY
DATE:
SUNDAY
DATE:
DOOMSDAY
DATE:

MONTH:

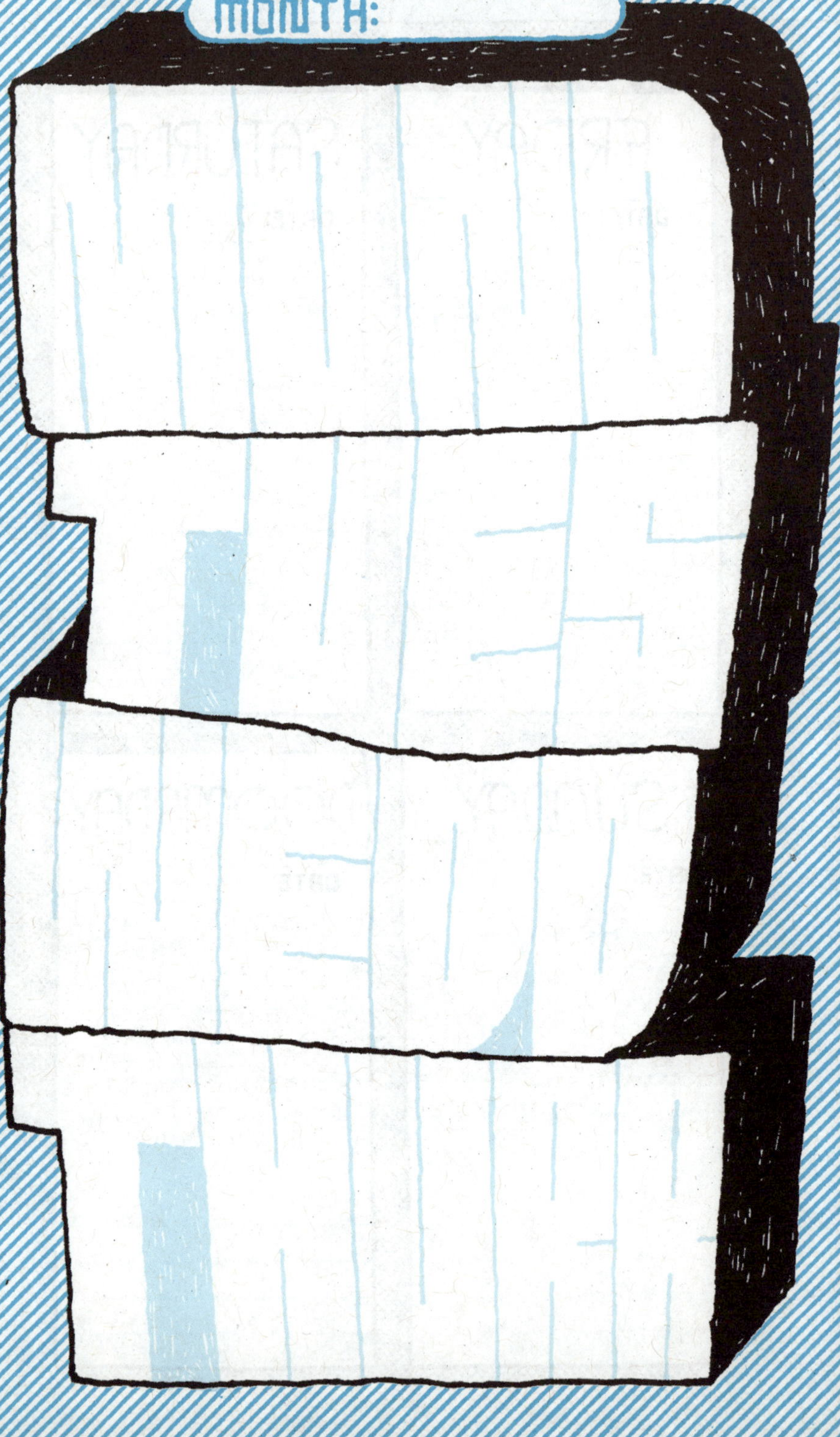

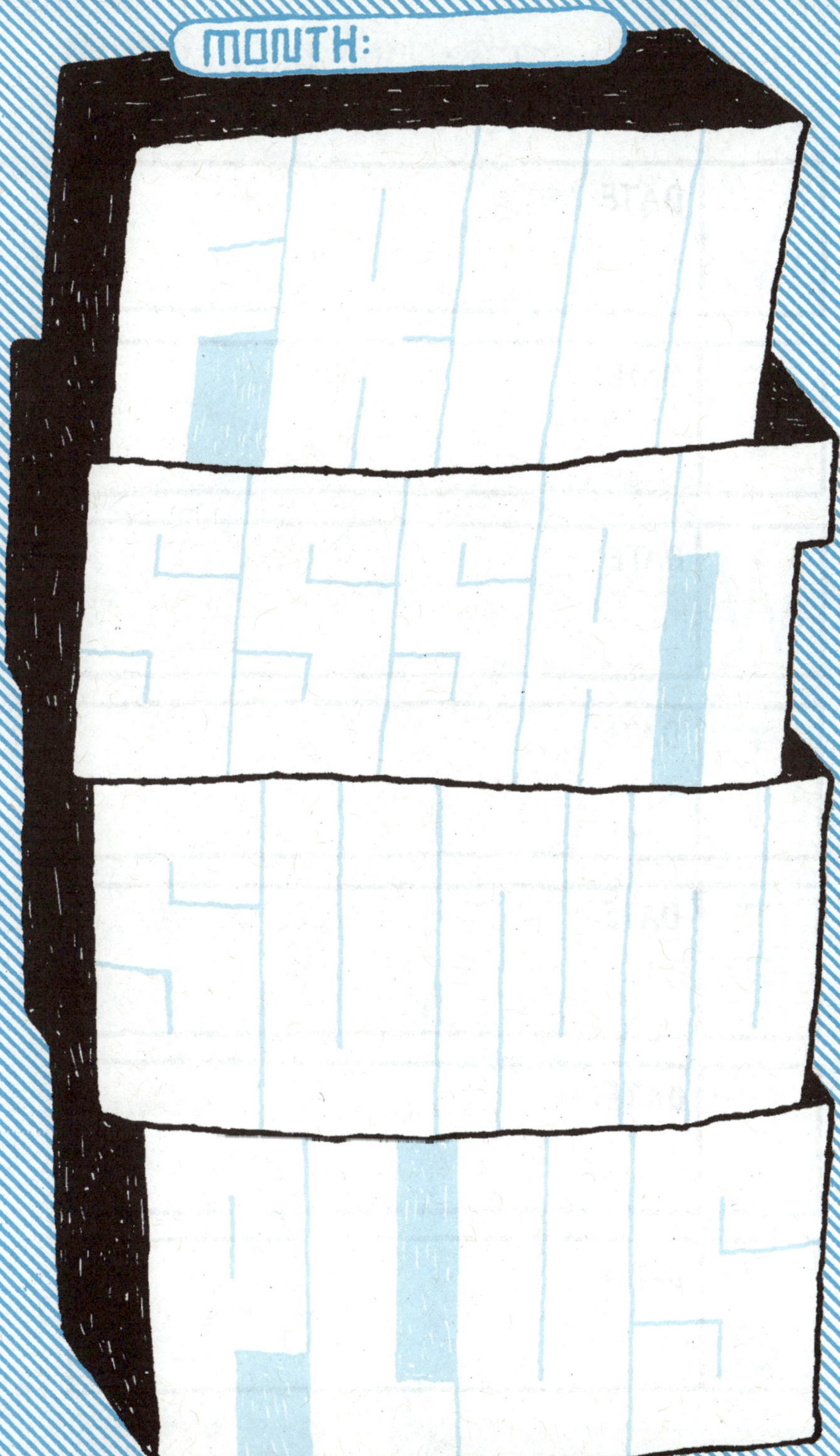
MONTH:

QUICK WEEK PREDICTIONS

M	DATE:
T	DATE:
W	DATE:
T	DATE:
F	DATE:
S	DATE:
S	DATE:

ANDREW HOOD

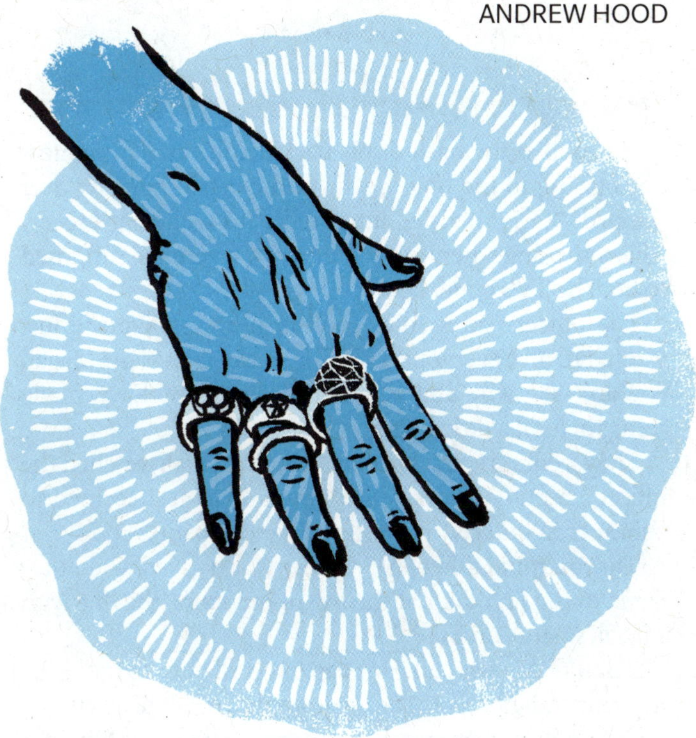

A Place for Everything

IN THE LIVING ROOM all the drawers had been yanked out and emptied. Heaps of instruction manuals for electronics they no longer owned and exhausted batteries they had not been sure how to throw out environmentally. Empty plastic film canisters, dead pens, and elastics. Coupons and take-out menus. They had unpacked the last of the boxes that weekend, and seeing this mess on the floor now, Magali wondered why her dad had packed away all that junk drawer stuff. You don't track in all the crap from an old home into a new one.

He rubbed the back of his neck helplessly now, almost apologizing to the officer, who had her pen hanging over her pad. "Gee," her dad fumfured. "It's really hard to say what's missing when everything's not where it's supposed to be. The TV's gone, I guess. Obviously."

The officer had a shiny look in her eyes like she just wanted to give everyone a big hug, make it all okay. Magali couldn't see why she couldn't. That might have made things at least a little better.

They went upstairs. Lagging behind, Magali watched the officer's bum—Officer Walsh's bum. It almost seemed to shimmer in the navy polyester of her cop pants.

"Do you mind if I go in?" Officer Walsh asked when they came to the first door at the top of the stairs, the one with Magali's name on it.

"I don't," Magali said. Her dad lingered outside the room a moment, before wandering down the hall to his own.

Seeing it all scattered in a mound on her bed like that, Magali was embarrassed of her underwear, the plainness and whiteness of it. To have Officer Walsh see. But then she began to wonder about the ones Officer Walsh had. Whether or not they were also police issued, like her pants, and her socks, and her ponytail.

A five disc CD player had been taken, with both discs of the White Album, Shostakovich's 9th in E minor, and two boy pop bands Magali only listened to with headphones on inside it. Her computer was gone also; her phone; and an old hot pepper jar full of loonies that would have been enough for an electric guitar in a few months.

"Cool room," Officer Walsh said. "Nice and big."

"It's the master," Magali said. "My dad took the small one."

Officer Walsh fingered a tack in the edge of the Abbey

Road poster over Magali's desk. "You like the Beatles?"

"I love the Beatles," she said, though she didn't really like the Beatles. Like she didn't really like classical music, or the Eudora Welty, Virginia Woolf, or Alice Munro books she had on her shelf—all knocked onto the floor now—or the Cezanne and Modigliani posters she also had on her walls. They were likes she had taken from her mother, tastes she didn't understand, which she understood would eventually set her apart from people, make her special, tastes which she hoped to soon love without pretending.

"Want to see something?" Magali blurted out like a breath she'd been holding.

"Sure."

Splayed on the bed was a naked plastic doll with a lazy eye. Its head twisted off without much effort. Two shakes and a tangle of jewellery fell into Magali's palm.

Officer Walsh smiled at Magali. "Very smart," she said.

The necklaces she balled up in her fist, but the rings Magali slid on. She liked the way they hung on her fingers. The extra room she would grow into.

Officer Walsh held Magali by the tips of her fingers and admired the rings: a wedding ring, two amethysts that had been her grandmother's, and an opal ring—her mother's birth stone—which spiralled with blues, purples, and greens like some underwater storm. There were no rings on Officer Walsh's fingers.

"They're beautiful," Officer Walsh said, smiling again. Feeling the flash of heat in her cheeks, Magali yanked her hands away.

In his small bedroom at the end of the hall they found Magali's dad standing in the mess like he was lost. Papers and clothes were everywhere. Magazines had been scattered and spread all over the floor, the nightgown and underwear ones that were still coming in the mail, addressed to her mom. Clay shards from pots her mom had made were all over the bedroom floor, in no way indicating the lovely, careful things they had been.

"To think," her dad said, "of someone coming in here and assigning some stupid value to something and never even imagine the actual value of it..." He sounded like he was trying to make himself cry.

Magali took a few steps towards him, stopping when her foot was down on one of the magazines. Pivoting a bit, she cleared a sock from the cover. Why anyone would wear their underwear in the woods was beyond her. At the corner was a rectangle of white paper, with their new address on it, and her mom's name still.

Magali saw Officer Walsh stare right at one of those magazines, one of his magazines, and then look professionally back at Magali's dad, who was standing by his dresser, looking so stupid. He hiccuped.

"Can you tell whether anything's been taken?" Officer Walsh asked, sliding her pad into her back pocket.

"Oh, I'm sure something," he said.

Feeling them beginning to slide, Magali made a fist to keep her rings from falling off.

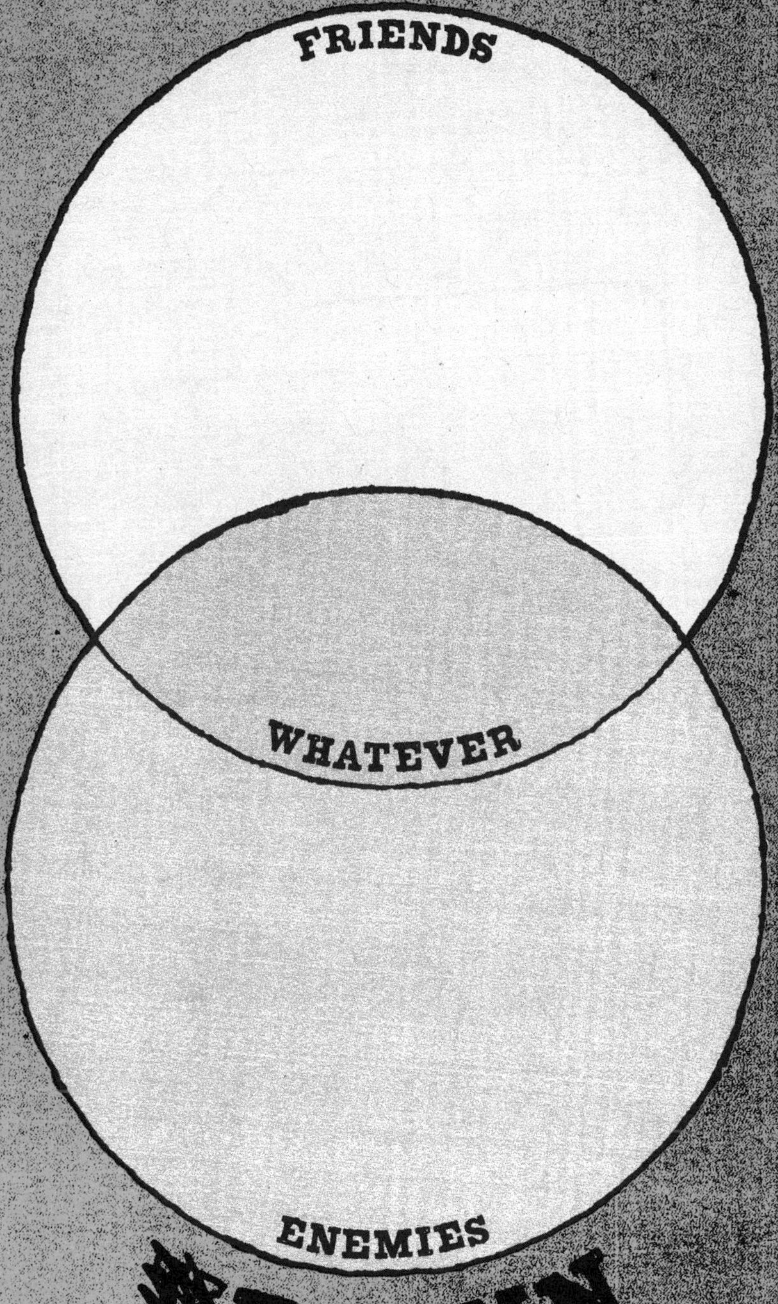

FRENN DIAGRAM

MON

MONTH: DATE:

TUES

MONTH: DATE:

WED

MONTH: DATE:

THUR

MONTH: DATE:

FRI

MONTH: DATE:

SAT

MONTH: DATE:

SUN

MONTH: DATE:

ETC

WHATEVER:

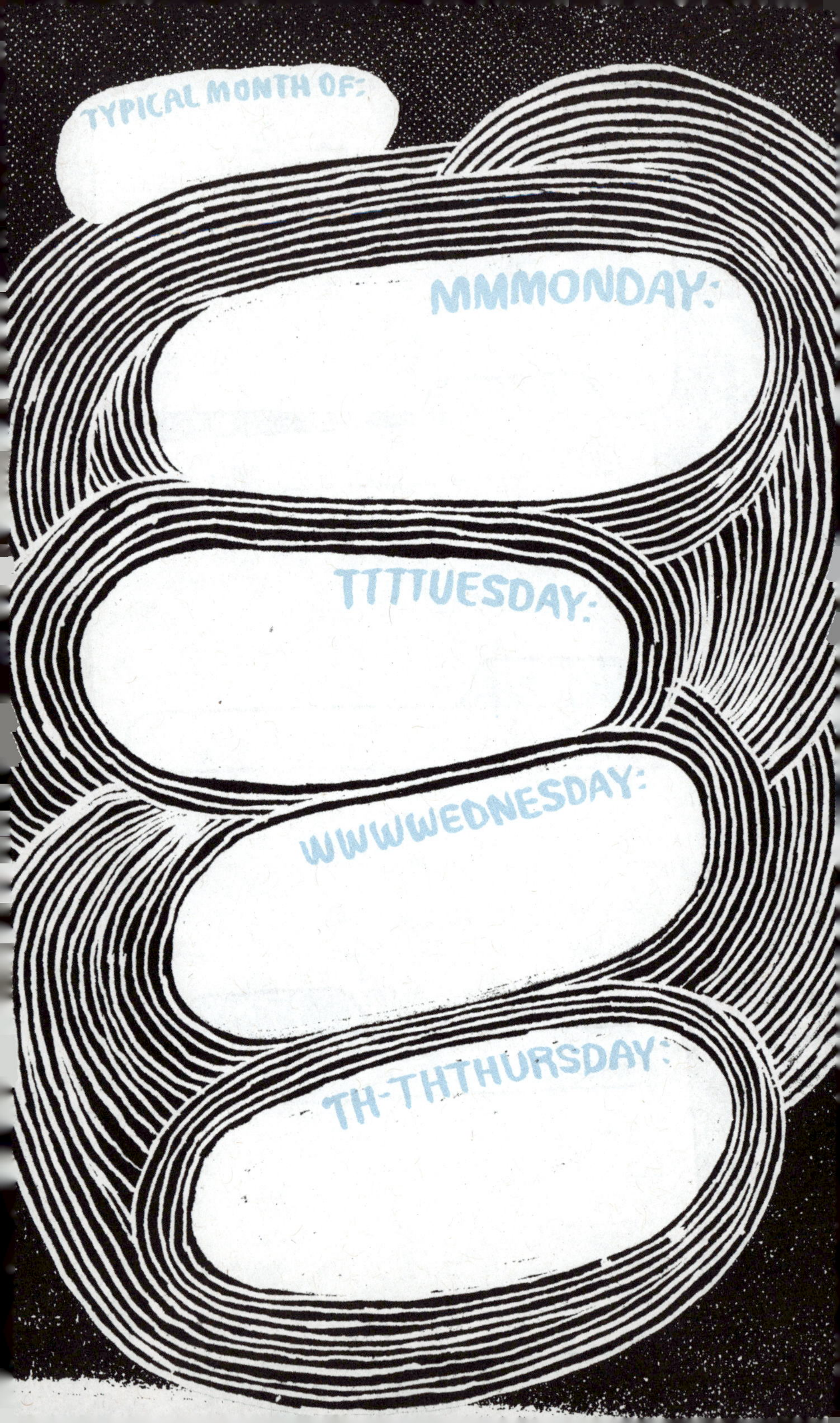
TYPICAL MONTH OF:
MMMONDAY:
TTTTUESDAY:
WWWWEDNESDAY:
TH-THTHURSDAY:

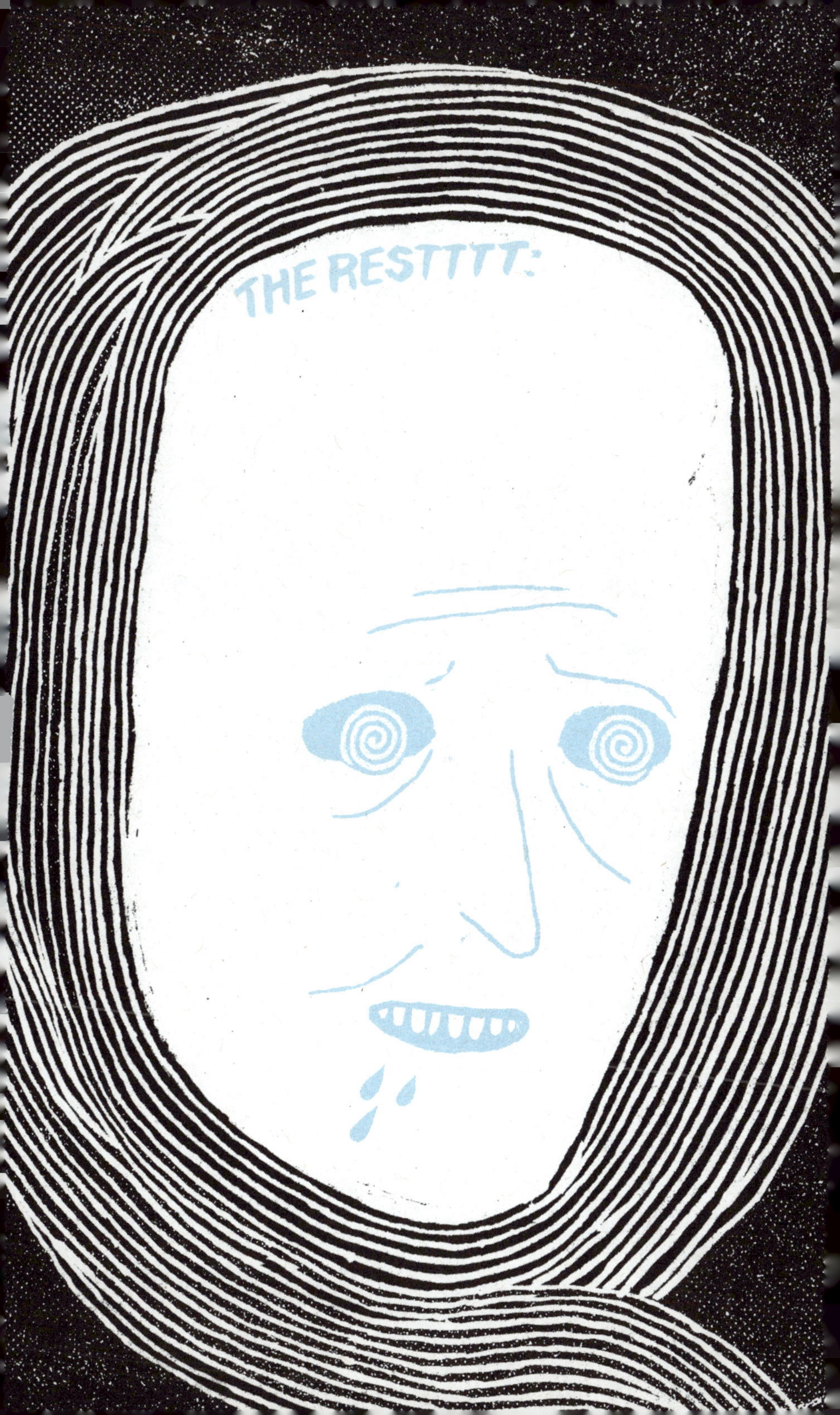
THE RESTTTT:

DOODLER

KATIE HEINDL

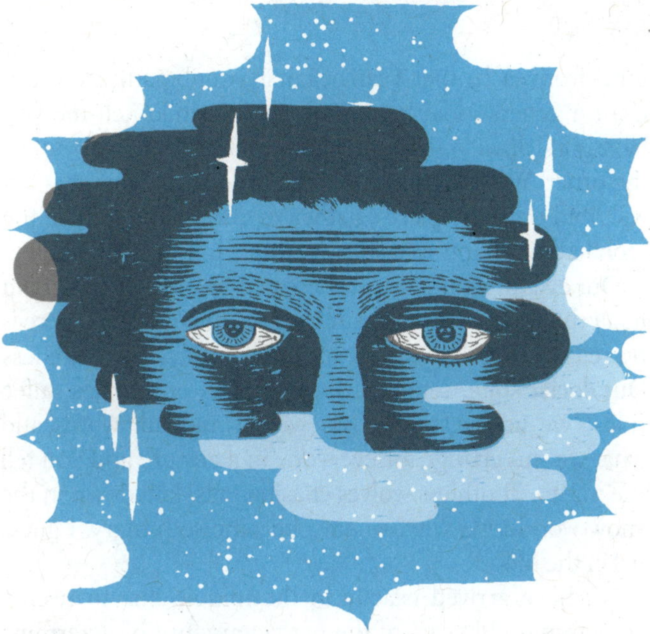

To The Teeth

OUR HEADS ARE ABOUT THE SAME SIZE. If I could steer my bike with no hands I am fairly sure we'd ride the same. We have the same things inside and without the terrible episodes we have put each other through it would be impossible to hear each other's keening rage in the night. You say they gave it all up for us. You say for me to be this open they had to become that closed. They shut down and funnelled in some crude, selfless way, all that energy and hope, into us. We are rabid dreams. We are going to end up burned up on back roads tens of thousands of miles from home, only a few miles from each other. I can hear it in your breath, staggered from a generational habit. You choke, smile, tell me you have gone down 4 sizes and I know neither of us will outlive the other. We will go at the same time and whoever is left will hold onto the pieces, gather so quietly and handle the scorched remnants as if still breathing, but that will be all.

Our eyes are the same washed out blue and we can't help it, all the ways we feel the undertow. On good days there is no reason to go anywhere and on bad days there are less. Our social state, removed from us, but our smiles, infectious. We underestimate our weight and our words and what we can change for everyone in a gesture and you tell me not to. Toothless wolves chasing tails, laid down in the snow wondering why we have become so hungry. I guess it's in the blood.

We have arrived exactly in the middle due to twenty-something-odd years of the perfect amount of determination. We sometimes lose the sense of what that means, we have swallowed it whole. I imagine terrible things happening to you as you disappear beside a garbage truck.

What incredible speed! We operate at such incredible speed! The take, the give, the velocity is extreme and the violence that comes seems hardly a surprise. We edge along the outsides, hand over hand, low and searching. We steady ourselves or just grow to a point where all the shaking seems to even out and we shake ourselves solid. In us there is a better wish, a clear quality that is hard to get at. We lay tight in times, sucking all the air out until our lungs burned and our fever was something to take out along with us. All the blood ran backwards and we were privy to it, thinner than ozone but with the same rare and used-up quality. We are so warm at our best, the best we have is holding onto each other. We swell gold and breathe glad, our health comes from each other and how is it we forget. Our finger prints, smudged and layered all over everyone we know, as if there will be nothing left of us than what we've left on each other. All the choices we have to make seem too loud to be any sort of sound.

Pinned against a sedan I stall and scoot and my heel clicks the driver's door and I feel breathless grinning, stand on my pedals and strain to catch up. I imagine everyone on the sidewalk is smiling as they watch and clasp their hands and admit what good siblings we make.

"Now there is work," They nod, "now there go two, against all odds, who admit defeat and will shut the blinds and know they at least have a synchronized heart."

They are so admiring! As we speed and swerve and I stop at the lights to fall into you and you beat my back and I cringe and the light changes and the people around us have no idea what is happening. What if the only reason we are here is for each other?

At least I am assured that in what I did and you didn't and what you did and was too illegal for me, we have carefully cultivated the exact same experiences and can fill in the blanks where we need to. When you were stealing prescription medication from seniors at the golf course I was at sleep-away camp afraid to sleep for fear of spontaneously combusting. The day I found out you had tuberculosis I was pulled from a science lab and spent it in the principal's office crying my eyes out with no real idea of what any of it even meant. I missed woodshop and maybe kept an arm. You are forever contagious.

Our mile markers are in blood. All our blood is everywhere, think of all the places we have left our blood by now!

In South Carolina tidal pools after slicing our fingers open on sun-hot and bloated sea urchins, shredding knees and left to bake dry and hardly leave a trace on red Nevada rocks, just more rusted fodder for the desert. Bitten by macaws in San Diego, snagged low by wild blueberry bushes at the top of Mount Washington.

We are the best and worse of what has happened to each other and we are going to be the same foul examples of what is to come. Our teeth and our dissonance, our bad hearts and our spite. Our best ideas and our worst stomach pangs. Our ferocity is never feigned. Our best nights, our most true examples of each other, when we strangle a turkey by the bottle neck and jump off high-up things into people we don't know. When we are crude and savage and snarl with lips curled back at preposterous angles and laugh so hard we spit and feel the weight of every person in the room, their hearts and their tenderness and how they are sorry. When we rush and force and finally do not stop to take account until we are under cars. When we are at our best.

You are my best. You are what I am capable of. You are my truancy and you are my weight in salt and in suns. You are where I am going and you are where I have been and when I close my eyes we are running at each other's throats and I am glad for your blood, singing and boiling, in mine.

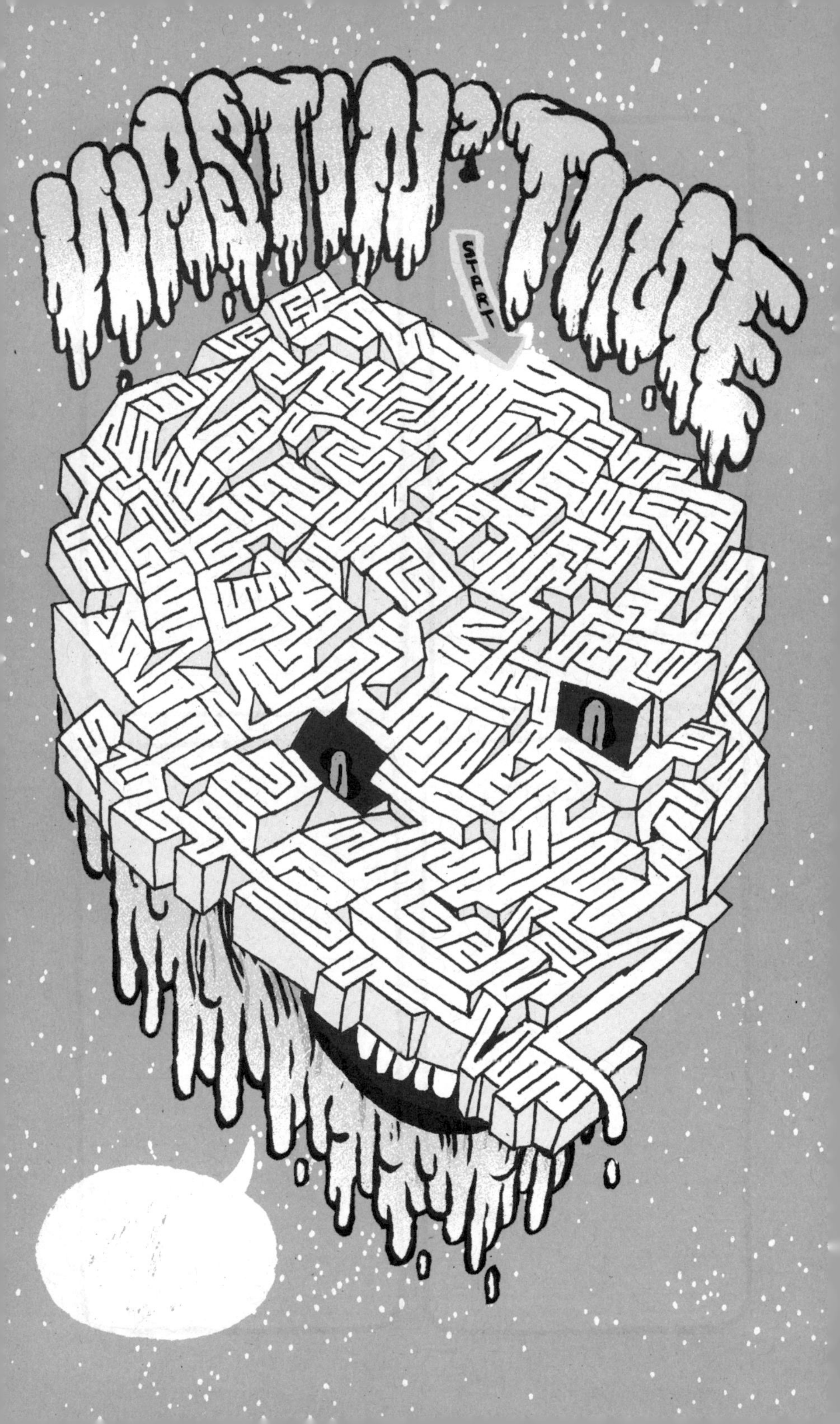
WASTIN' TIME
START

MONDAY

DATE:

TUESDAY

DATE:

WEDNESDAY

DATE:

THURSDAY

DATE:

FRIDAY

DATE:

SATURDAY

DATE:

SUNDAY

DATE:

NOTES

~~DATE~~:

A MONTH CALLED

MONDAY DATE

TUESDAY DATE

WEDNESDAY DATE

THURSDAY DATE

FRIDAY DATE

SATURDAY DATE

SUNDAY DATE

EXTRA

MINIWEEK

M DATE:

T DATE:

W DATE:

T DATE:

F DATE:

S DATE:

S DATE:

JOSHUA TIBBETTS

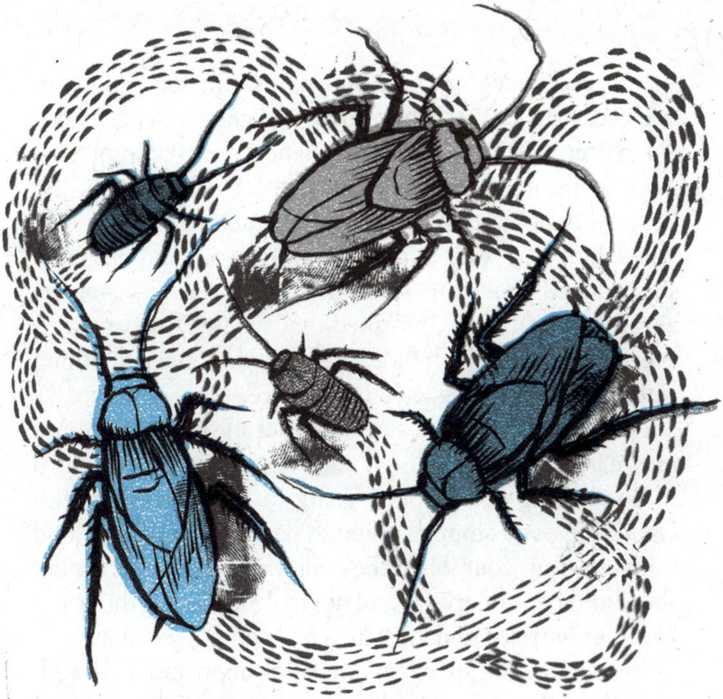

Afghanistan The Unconquerable

DEVILISHLY DELIGHTFUL IN A RED COCKTAIL DRESS, with hair that piled on top of itself like a double-decker strawberry ice cream cone, and her second to none push-up bra that stabbed you right in the groin while shrieking *Oooh-la-la*!

The problem with those semi-formal get-togethers is that they always skewed too far toward the formal. Blinders were up as regards any man exhibiting the t-shirt and jeans combination of tried tested and true tradition, especially a man as regrettably forgettable as you unfortunately are in the department of looks.

But you kept coming and you kept seeing her here there and everywhere. You kept coming and getting your knocks. No matter how formal a shape you beat yourself into.

Afghanistan refused to be defeated by the British, the Ruskies, the Macedonians. Unconquerable.

She looked at you, and she talked to you, and one time she touched your arm. Thought it was flirtation as materialization of crushing. Informed that she was that way with everyone. A coquettish individual. It didn't mean anything when she acknowledged your existence.

I have it on very good authority that she is not interested in you in that way.

Good thing you stopped going to semi-formal parties. Good thing you stopped going to parties altogether. Good thing you quit your job at the mall where she shops for her shoes and her underwear and her makeup. Good thing you have not replaced said job with a fresh one. Good thing you sit in your bedbug apartment morning noon and night with the lights off and the curtains down and the computer feeding porn into your eye sockets via gamma rays or some such. Good thing you don't have to see her anymore. Good thing.

I, for one, am glad that you have found a way to move past this girl. As your landlord, I feel I can say that I was getting bummed about your unhealthy obsession with that rubicund bimbo. I hated to see you beating yourself up, inflating yourself with hope only to spring a leak and end up flat, empty, and down on the ground. No use in obsessing over something you can never have.

There is still the matter of the rent however.

Again, it's great that you quit your job, if your job was going to keep her as a fixture in your life on a semi-weekly basis. It's great for your mental health. But the funny thing about mental health is how it always works in direct opposition with the acquisition and dispensation of monetary funds. Inverse proportion, with your mind on the y axis and the money you owe me on the well you get the idea.

Look, we've known each other a long time, right? Go way back. Remember flipping Coleman off in grade ten shop class? A hoot. A bona-fide hoot. And those memories will always be special. When this super-duper fine-and-dandy partially infested apartment opened up at a moment in time that coincided with your getting dumped and kicked out of that other redhead's one bedroom place, I hooked you up. Right away. First person I thought of.

I apologize. The time that coincided with your getting dumped and kicked out of *Leah's* one bedroom place.

Can I be frank? You give in too quickly. Fall to pieces. It's called indecision and it's detrimental to your well-being. You cannot just sit here in your picturesque and slightly bugged-up accommodations and expect life to get any better. You have to go out into the wide world and grab the bull by the horns, as the saying goes, and shake it and gore it and bleed it out for all its worth. Gore it like you're the one who's the bull, and the bull is just I don't know a weak little desert bunny I guess. A river of blood could be yours, a river of bloody cash flow goodness. Because rent was due two weeks ago and friendship or not this won't stand.

You have to be strong. Like a mighty nation. Afghanistan refused to be defeated by the British, the Ruskies, the Macedonians. Unconquerable.

Yes, she was your Afghanistan, but that's just it, you can be Afghanistan too. Be impossible to surmount. An underdog country of one. Sure you've seen some bad times, you've had your personal Talibans and tribulations, but you can take solace in the fact that you are unbeatable. A mighty nation, no matter what anyone says.

A tendency toward bad breath. A tendency to wear sleeveless tops and dresses while displaying a European density of armpit hair. A tendency to laugh at her own jokes when everyone else is crickets. She's not the tops. She's just a redhead, and you have some Freudian foul-up in your circuitry where you saw a little red-haired girl's little pink panties when you were a little five year-old and ba-boom your entire lovemap was charted for good and all. Just programming. No different from your laptop there, with its—what is that, anal three-way? No different from anal three-way.

Okay, cry. You owe me my money, and nothing is going to change the fact that you pay me money to live in this craphole, not the other way around. Maybe my job isn't glamorous, maybe it's not what I wanted out of life, but at least I got one. You look down on me for being a slimy old landlord, but you're a big nothing. So suck it up. Starting now. No woman is worth this. They're just primates. The carpets don't even match the drapes. Or so I've heard.

So I slept with her. Big deal.

So I'm still sleeping with her. Big deal.

Maybe she doesn't like baby whinerpots who stew in their own seminal juices, pining over them from afar. Women like being desired, but only a little bit. Haven't you ever heard of hard to get?

Fine, get mad at me. Years of friendship, down the tube, waste of my life and yours, fine. I expect to see the money in two weeks time or you will be served an eviction notice.

No, I will not stop seeing her. Grow up and get a life.

It's just you and the roaches, together, alone.

If you'll excuse me, I have a date.

CLASSIC ACTIVITY PAGE

WRITE DOWN WHAT HAPPENED TODAY AND DRAW IT.

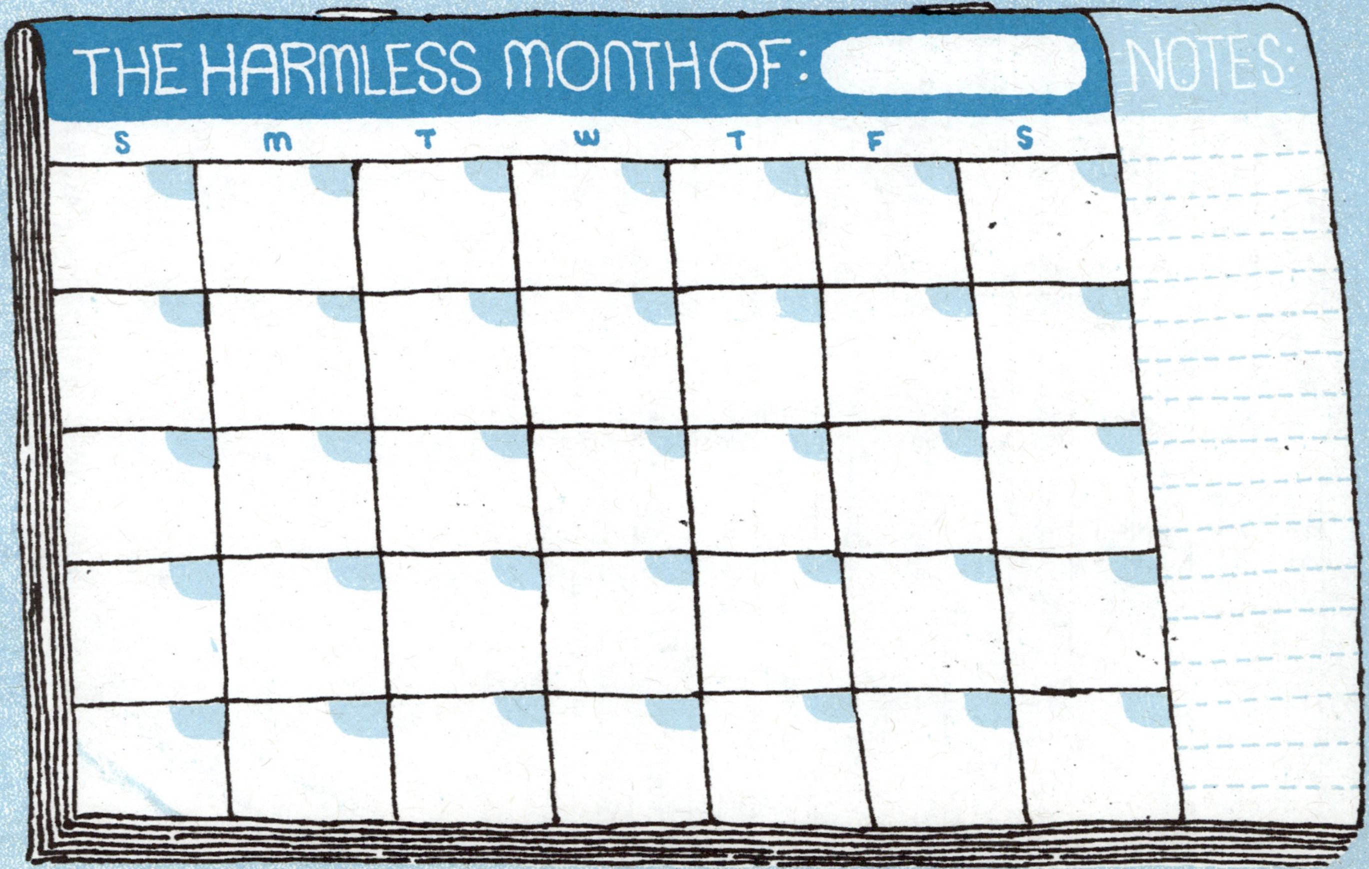
THE HARMLESS MONTH OF:
NOTES:
S
M
T
W
T
F
S

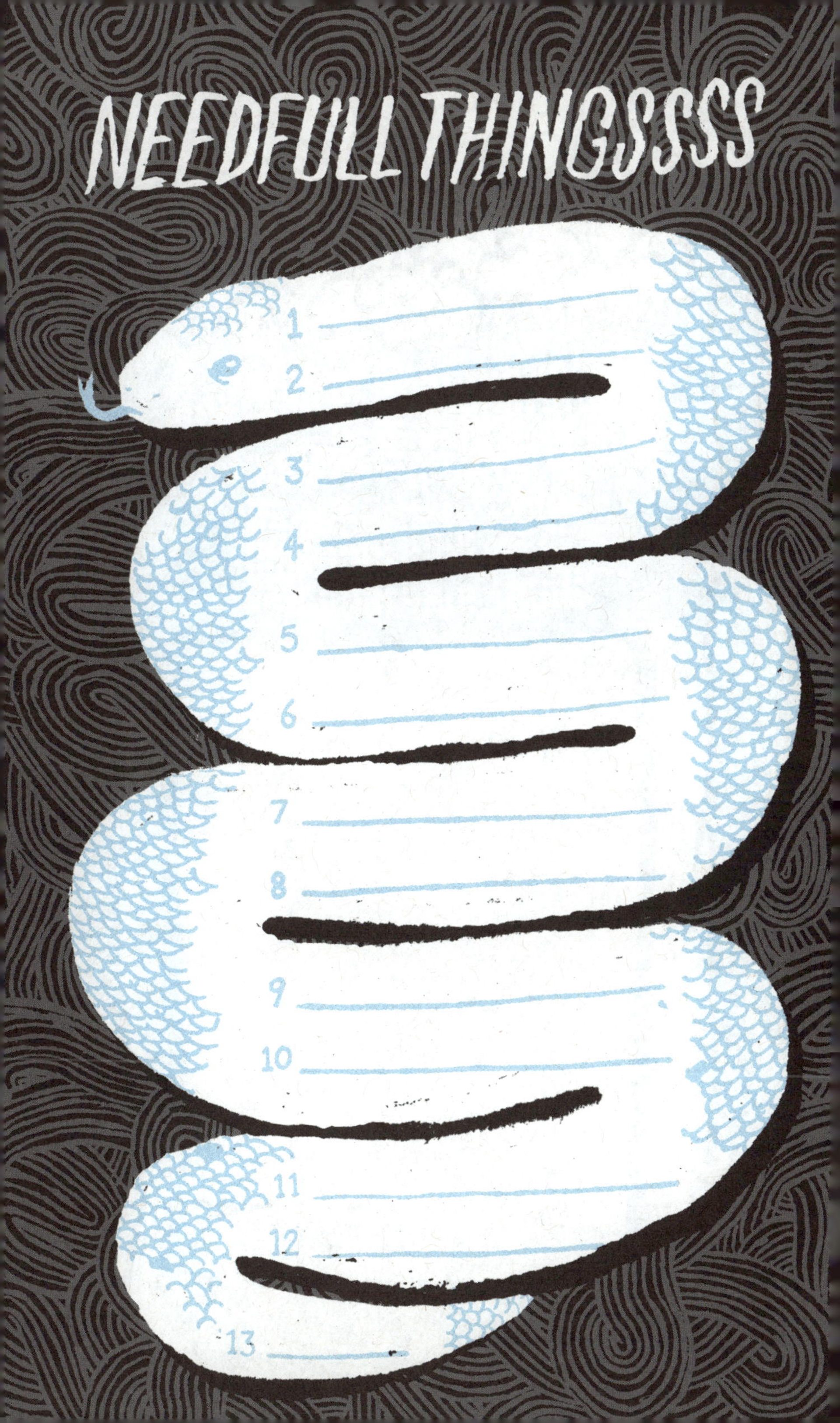
NEEDFULL THINGSSSS
1
2
3
4
5
6
7
8
9
10
11
12
13

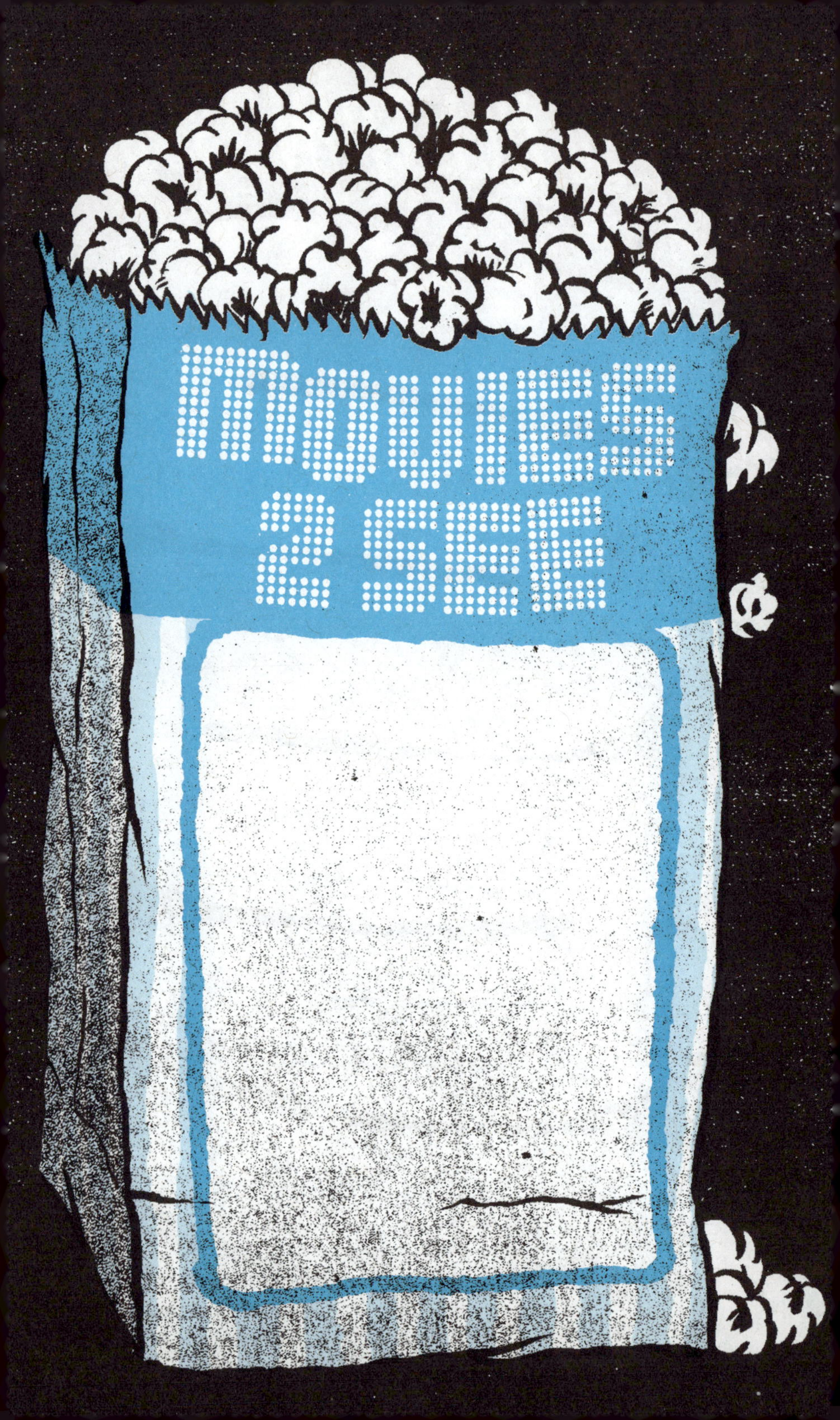
MOVIES
2 SEE

SA

FR

TH

WE

TU

MO

SU

“ ______________ ” THE MONTH

CHECK THIS MONTH:

SUN	MON	TUES	WED	THUR	FRID	SAT

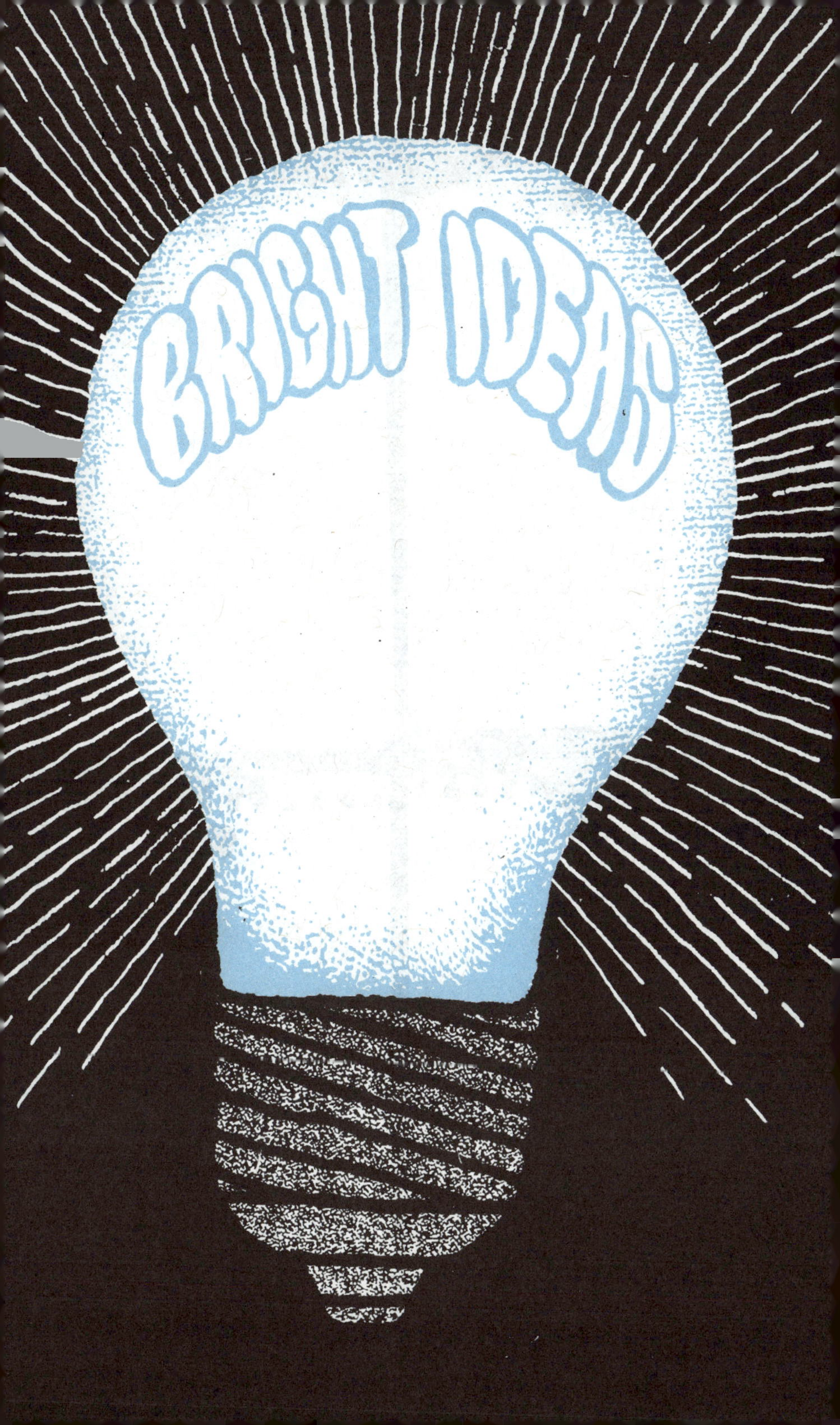
BRIGHT IDEAS

QUICK LISTS

SCOTT HERDER

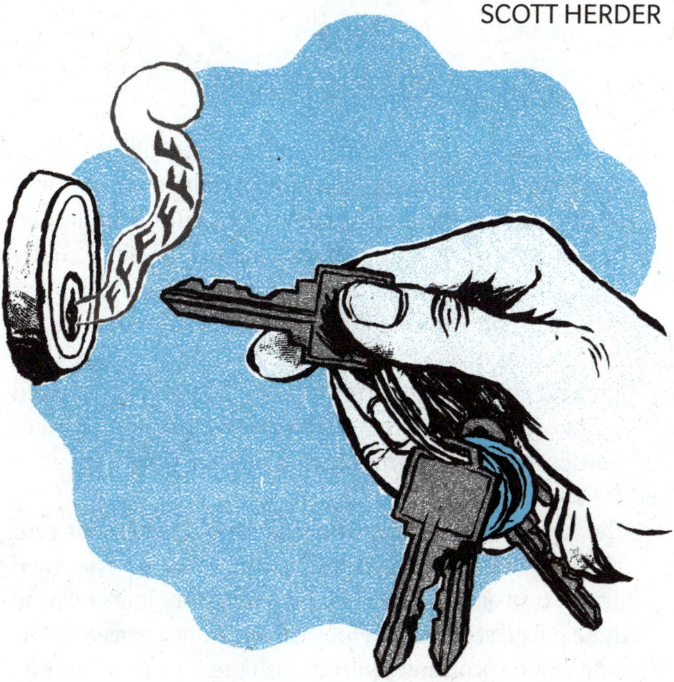

Strike Flat the Thick Rotundity

I LOCKED THE DOOR TO MY HOUSE just as the breeze lit, my keys jangling nervously as the afternoon warmth began to wane. I have kept each of my keys for years, despite my gradual forgetting of which ones went to which locks. As my feet dropped from my doorstep the wind picked up, combing my hair down or ruffling it up depending upon the direction I chose to face. A warm draft at last, and it was tugging at the bottom of my jacket and cuffs of my pants, springing movement and alluding to direction. And always angling upwards, it seemed, as if culling each object of the world to its own designed rendering. My keys sat heavily after I let them drop back into my jacket pocket.

The afternoon was beginning to send the sun's rays at an

increasing horizontal. Their beams glanced off the shoulders of great, dominating machinery that stood still in a slouching pose in the midst of new mountains of rocks and dirt. This was to be some condominium housing. Along the lurching arm of one of the excavators stood several black birds. Three birds silhouetted against the sky behind them, looking magisterial over the construction site, their orders and chirps lost to me in the puffing breaths of wind between us. I kept walking, my hands in each jacket pocket, one absently clutching my keys, the other slowly cracking each of its knuckles.

The next block had on one side an old, well-kept cemetery, and a nicely groomed park on the other. Each seemed a curious translation of the sobriety of nature in its relation to these paved streets. Carefully carved stones placed neatly in long rows, sprouting up from lush grass to stand among solemn oaks. Park playgrounds with softly standing ladders and swings, circled by groomed pathways. Havens for life, artificial heaths.

At the next corner, the solid hand across the street held steady, and two other young men waited to cross.

—Ah, tonight will be good, man. Last day of work, and I'm going to celebrate.

—Can I shower and change at your place? I don't want to wear these clothes out later. This shirt stinks, and I want to look good.

—Oh, yeah. Sure.

—I think it's going to storm tonight. I should have taken my coat.

I wondered about their clothes: loose workout shorts and shirts, and one of them held a frisbee in his hand. They looked to have just come from the park, perhaps having made a game of extravagant performance each time they caught the disc that the other had thrown.

—Damn, yeah. Well, we can go back to your place first. We can drink there for a while before we hit other places. You know?

—Hmm? Okay, that works. Thanks.

I listened as we crossed the street—Oh God damn, I forgot my damn keys at work—though they stopped to wait again so that they might cross to our adjacent corner while I continued, their next words being whipped into noiselessness by sudden gusts that pasted my shirt close against my chest. Aside from those two, each of the streets were uncommonly empty of traffic and neighbourhood residents, although a few dim porch lights meekly lit the leaden air. The old bark of the trees seemed to deliberately stiffen at the growing gusts of wind, despite their thinning branches that all seemed to swat back and forth at each other. The sky was darkening, those beams from the horizon now replaced by waves of surging clouds, their hard shapes passing into one another to form an indistinguishable scroll of ashen story. Their series of patterns brought a sudden exposure to the spackled corners of the houses that lined each side of my padding steps.

A flock of leaves streamed across the street like a chorus call as my steps fell between afternoon and evening. I watched them follow one another, each tracing the path and coil of the one before it, but all billowing forward without a leader. Their dry song swept the pavement and was drawn up into the wisps of wind and over the curb to the sidewalk before me. There they dissipated, each spiralling to their own accord, leaving me still and bewildered. I stopped and bent my knees. One brown leaf was stuck in one brown shoelace. Its wilted vibrance made my shoe's brown look to have only a single dimension, a murky, flat drabness. These dead leaves, hands, drawing up order in the world.

Shuffling past several more driveways, I saw a woman in her front yard opposite my side of the street. The yard had a young tree planted awkwardly in its centre, shielded from the street by a flower garden dotted with anxious shrubs, and the woman was scuttling in and around them. A large new vehicle stood neatly in the driveway behind her. It was one of those oversized hybrids, and it crouched, looming behind the woman, emphasizing her fragility. She wore high-heeled shoes with a fine skirt and matching blazer. A heavy necklace and earrings swung about her, and a loose bracelet fell up and down her wrist with the push and pull of her rake, her neat hair being tousled about by both her movements and the crack-cheeked blasts. Working with her face downcast, she looked aged among the blowing shrubs. The sky darkened, a cold drop of rain was flung against my neck, and I let my shoes take me to the next street. The woman stood in her flower garden near the curb, raking leaves in the windstorm.

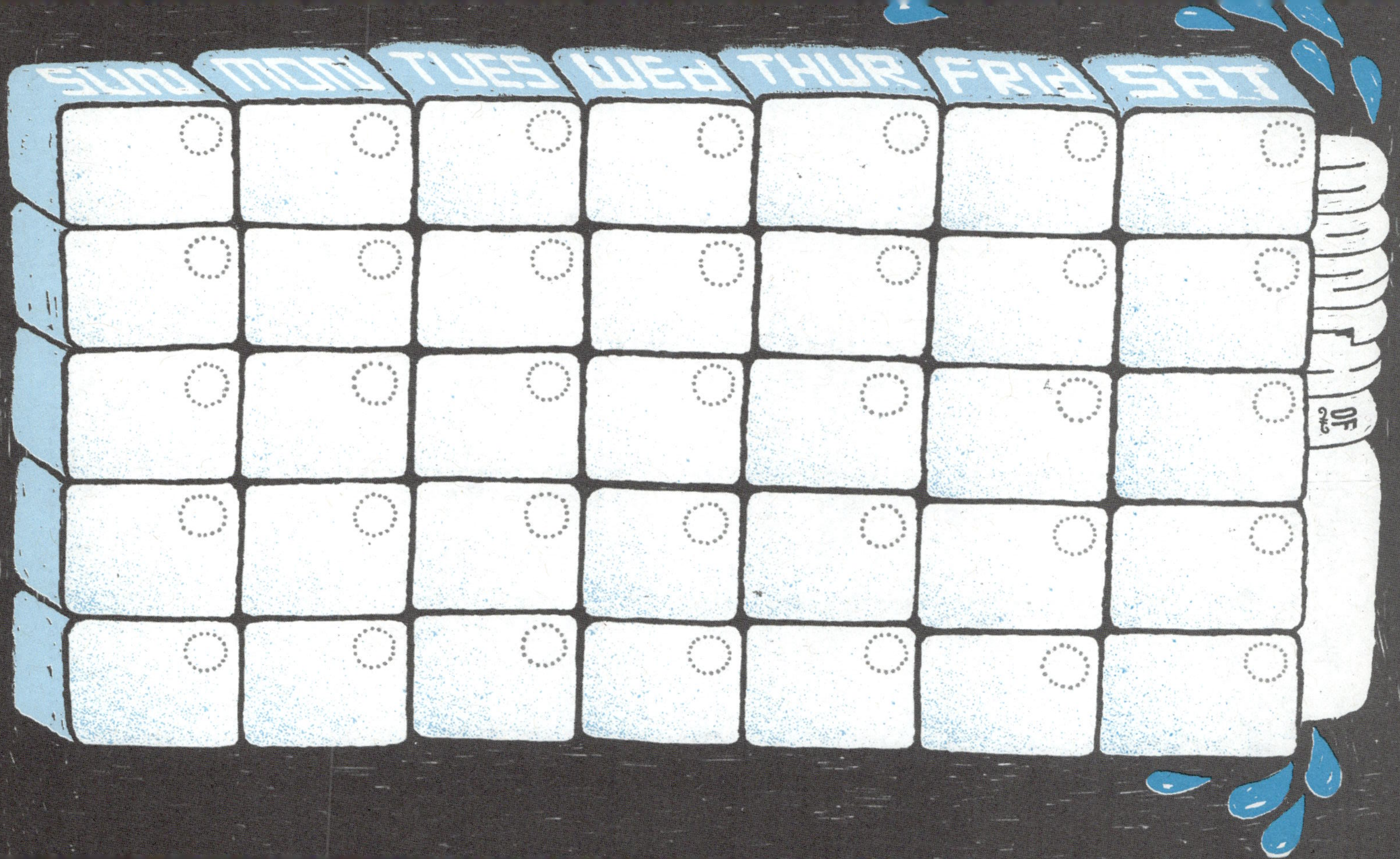
MONTH OF
SUN
MON
TUES
WED
THUR
FRI
SAT

THE MONTH OF:

SAT					
FRI					
THUR					
WED					
TUES					
MON					
SUN					

NAME	BIRTHDAY

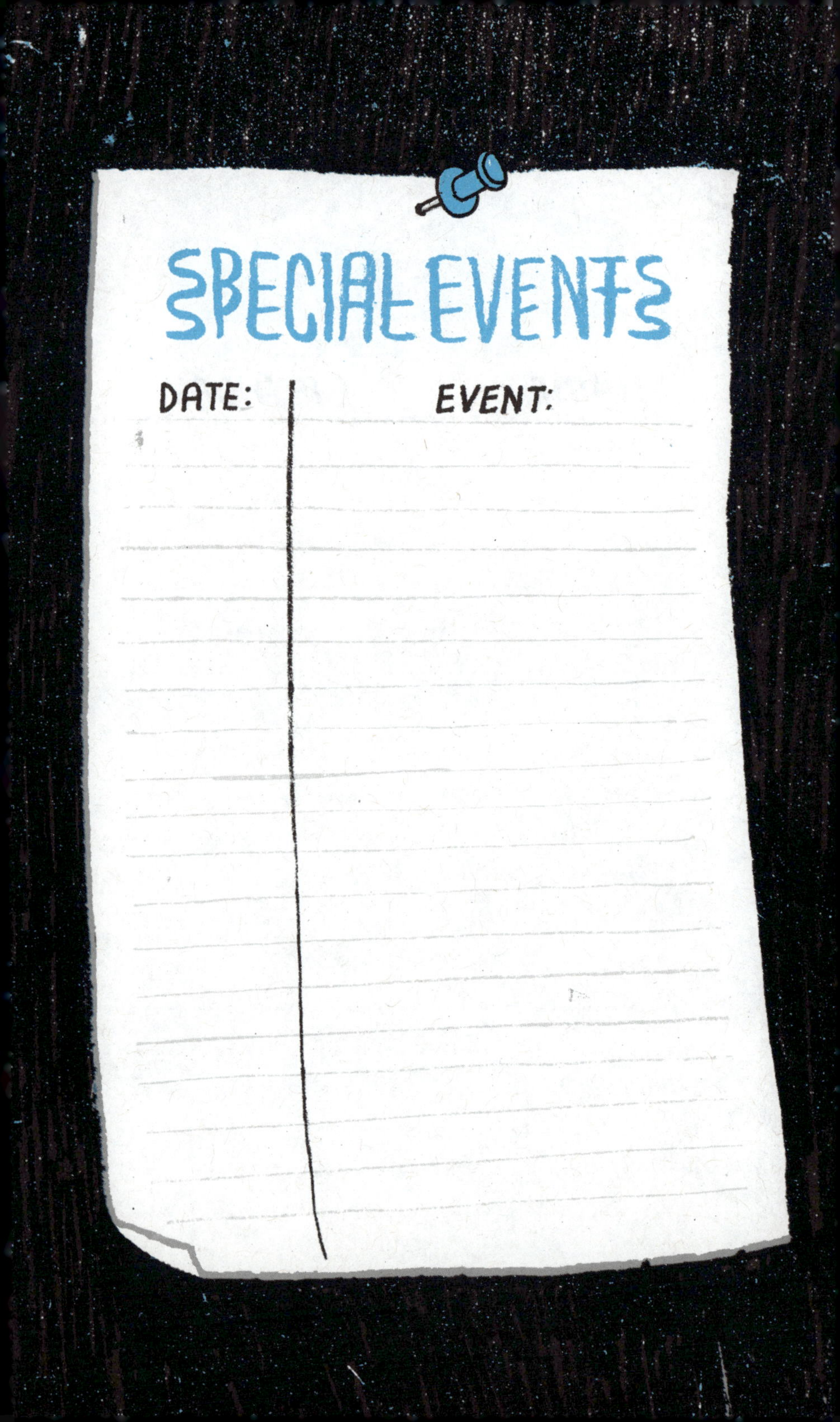
SPECIAL EVENTS
DATE:
EVENT:

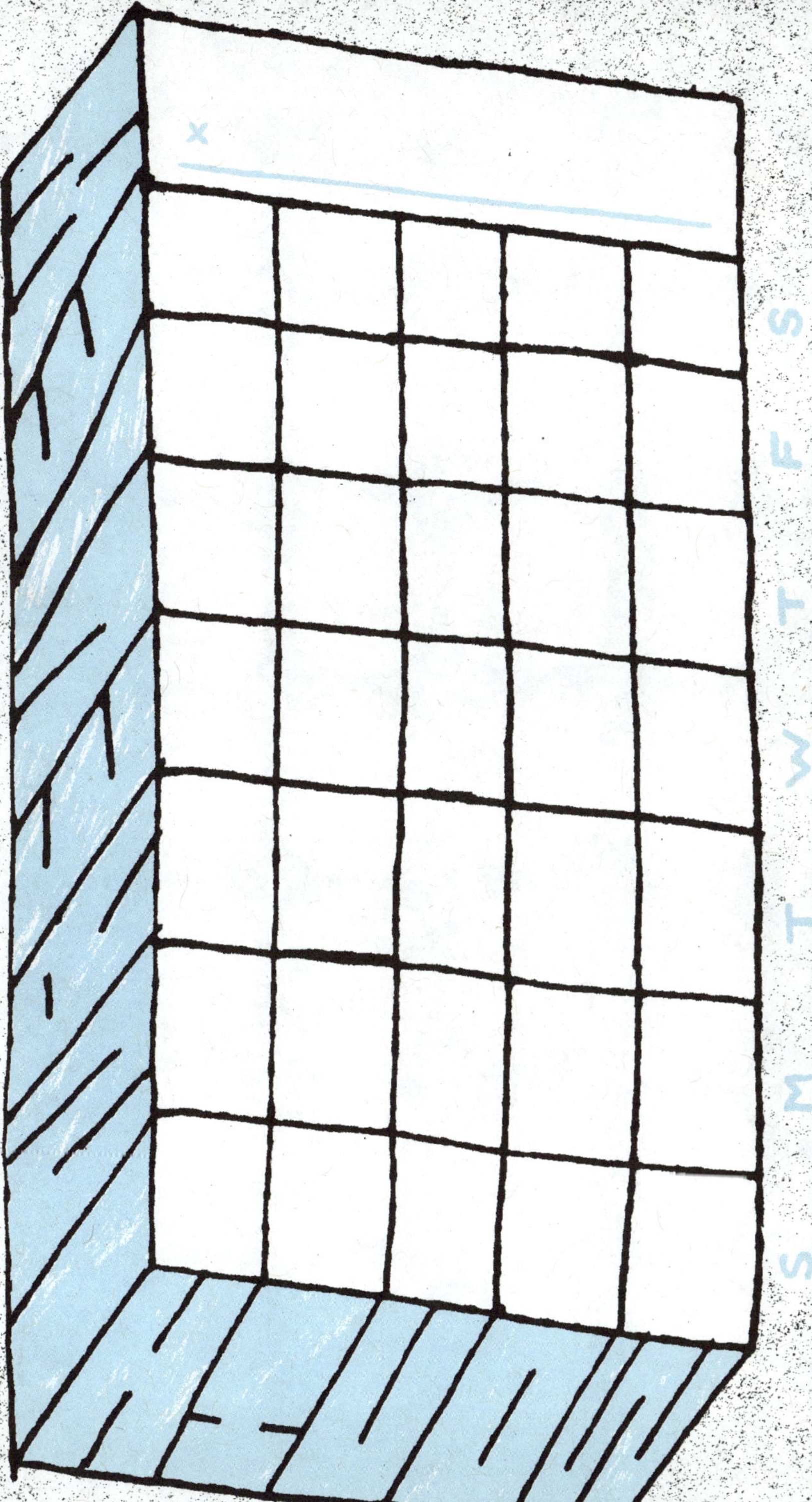
x
S M T W T F S

THE MINI MONTH OF ________

S	M	T	W	T	F	S

JENNER-BROOKE BERGER

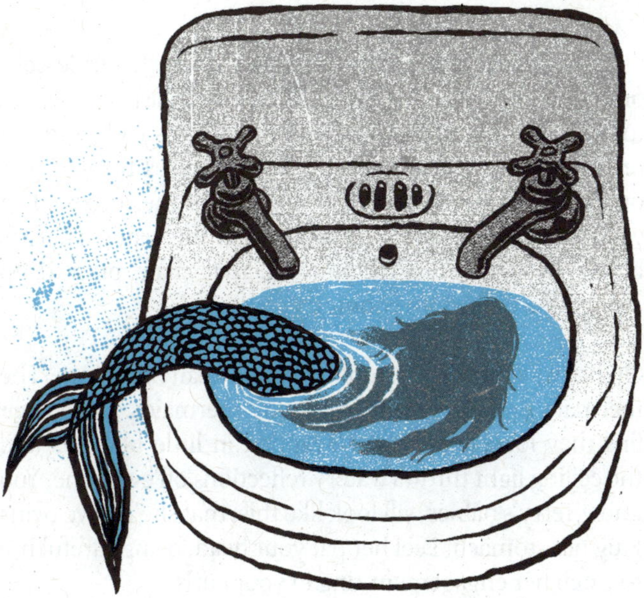

Negative Associations to Water/ Notes on Classical Conditioning re: Fear of Drowning

EMENDATIONS TO SUMMER 1994:

The red slip-covered chair is best, it has no arms. Slide it right into the small bathroom. Easier still, sidle it up to the sink. Mom and her pregnant friend talk in the living room. Terry is the least angry of Mom's women. She listens to you. She isn't stale, like Lorraine's perfume. Terry doesn't complain about men like Lorraine and Mom, despite her childhood. Terry does not question why she is unhappy, she seems to know. "In life you're punished for feeling pain, and rewarded for pleasure," Mom says.

In the bathroom, run the water over the iridescent orange fin of your mermaid doll. The splashes echo up toward the ceiling and back down. Sit cross legged in the red chair. Listen to Mom and Terry's voices through the open door, mixing in with the echoes of the mermaid. If you close the door you are alone with the water. There is barely enough room for you and that chair, pressed up against the bathroom counter.

On her way out, Terry stops by your Ocean bathroom. The mermaid doll came with two baby mermaids. With their fins they look like they're wrapped in little blankets and the ceiling light throws watery reflections off everyone. You know Terry's babies will look like this, that she'll have twins. Hug her stomach. Feel her pat your head, being careful not to catch her engagement ring in your curls.

After three weeks, be over the mermaid. Find two thin plastic dark green needles and learn to knit the tightest stitch. Everyday remember to be happy it is summer vacation. Don't watch tv at night when you can't fall asleep. Instead, glean everything you'll need to know from books. Soon you'll crochet, but not that soon. Don't knit a blanket for Terry's baby. It's a big project and will take you all summer; you only have one summer. Do it anyway. Make an afghan of blues: sea green, powder and baby and robin's egg blue, ultramarine and turquoise and cyan blue. The baby will really like it.

Ask your mom where Terry's been.

"She went to the hospital."

Clasp your small hands together, look down at them.

"She went to the hospital but she didn't have the baby."

Set down your knitting. Tell your Mom you don't get it. Across the room hear her say, "Terry went to have the baby but she didn't have a baby."

Don't think "twins." Don't do that. Don't let your eyes get so wide that they dry out and start to water to protect themselves. Don't picture Terry's twins. Don't see them swimming with orange fins, wrapped around them like blankets.

"The doctors told her to push out the baby, but there wasn't a baby. It was just air."

POST SCRIPT, AUTUMN '94:

Understand you are too old now to learn. Think about how it doesn't make sense in the fall. Swim lessons should happen in the summer, outside. Not in a place with no windows and dry heating. You are never warm enough to jump in. You never dry your hair for long enough. You catch a chill entering the crisp air with a wet head.

NOTES ON THE LAUNDRY ROOM, WINTER 1989:

"One day you'll be big, you'll have a job and kids of your own, or you'll be in University. Your room will be messy, and you'll just push Blanket onto the floor, and won't notice. You'll forget about Blanket, and never pick her up again."

She is crazy. You will never forget about Blanket.

"Just let me wash her. She's filthy and you're going to get sick. I can't afford to take time off work if you get sick."

But you know what's in there, the loud and angry sound of the machine as it fills with soapy water.

"You didn't seem to care about blanket when you took that pair of scissors to her."

Don't let guilt consume you. Your short-lived fascination with scissors is a natural curiosity, and didn't hurt anyone. Not really.

"Look, there's nothing in there." She lifts you from the waist, poising you over the lid of the machine. Don't look down into the thing. Close your eyes. Don't see the glass and metal. The violent long jagged weapons slamming up from each hole in the bottom of the washing tub. Don't scream. Think about the striking resemblance between Edward's scissor hands and the machine's weapons. Commend your imagination. Try to understand your imagination is separate from you. Understand years from now you will sit in a counsellor's office, in a mindfulness exercise. Your thoughts will be floating down a river in different colours in serif font and you will watch them. Some buoy in the current, get caught, spend longer there. Others throttle past you in the rapids. You are looking at your thoughts. Realize you are only looking at the *idea* of an armed washing machine. You are watching the idea of Terry's baby, stuck inside a pocket of air. You are watching an idea of the explosive fear of having your first swim teacher thrust your head under water, as you squirm and flail, until you hit your jaw on the perimeter of the cement pool. Emerging, choking on chemical water, with one less tooth. You are looking at the time your dad came upstairs, dark blood pouring from his wrists. You are only seeing the river and in the river is the image of you, saying to dad, "what happened to you," and him, there, bleeding, responding, "I was just fixing the washing machine."

ON FINALLY LEARNING TO SWIM:

Years later at Huy's cottage, when it's light and dark outside all at once, when no one is around, dip your head in over and over. Realize not the lifeguard, not anyone, is there to push you under. Huy teaches you to front crawl.

"Breath in."

"Now out."

You're not ready to dive. But you will be.

books to read
CHAPTER I

MONTH

S M T W T F S

VERY SIMPLY, THE MONTH OF:

SAT					
FRI					
THUR					
WED					
TUES					
MON					
SUN					

THIS MONTH IS:

SUN	MON	TUES	WED	THUR	FRI	SAT

KEEP IN TOUCH WITH FRIENDS

NAME	PHONE/EMAIL

IMPORTANT ADDRESSES

NAME	ADDRESS

KEEP IN TOUCH WITH FRIENDS

NAME	PHONE/EMAIL

IMPORTANT ADDRESSES

NAME	ADDRESS

KEEP IN TOUCH WITH FRIENDS

NAME	PHONE/EMAIL

MAKE YER OWN FUNNY PAGES

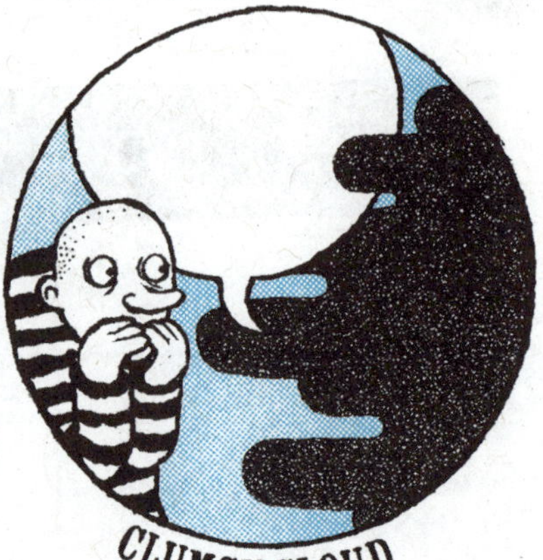

CLUMSY CLOUD

by ______________

CYCLOPS TWINS by ______________

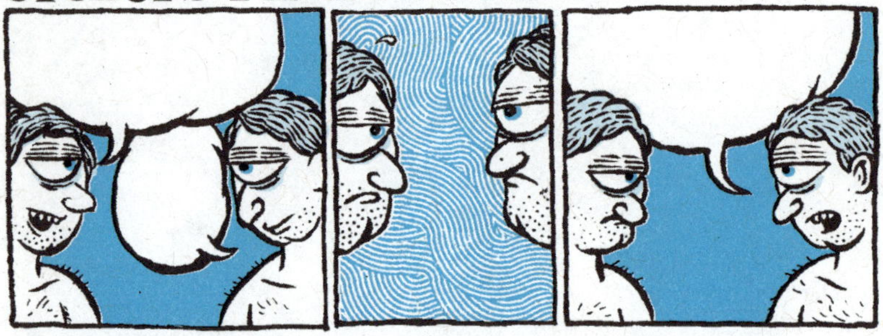

SECRET STUFF by ______________

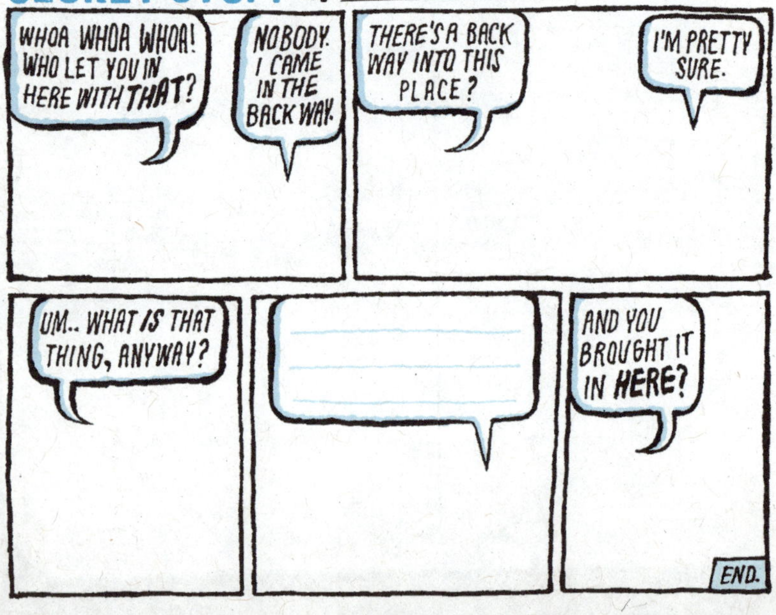

DO-GOODER

by ____________

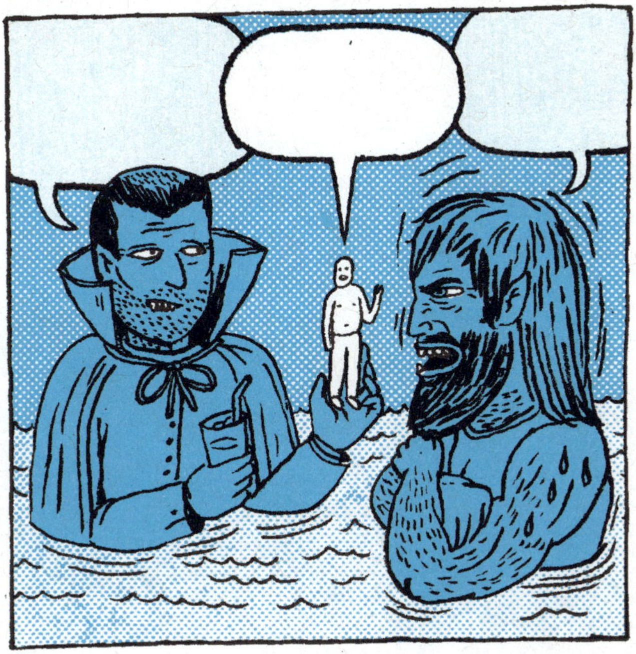

GARY by ____________

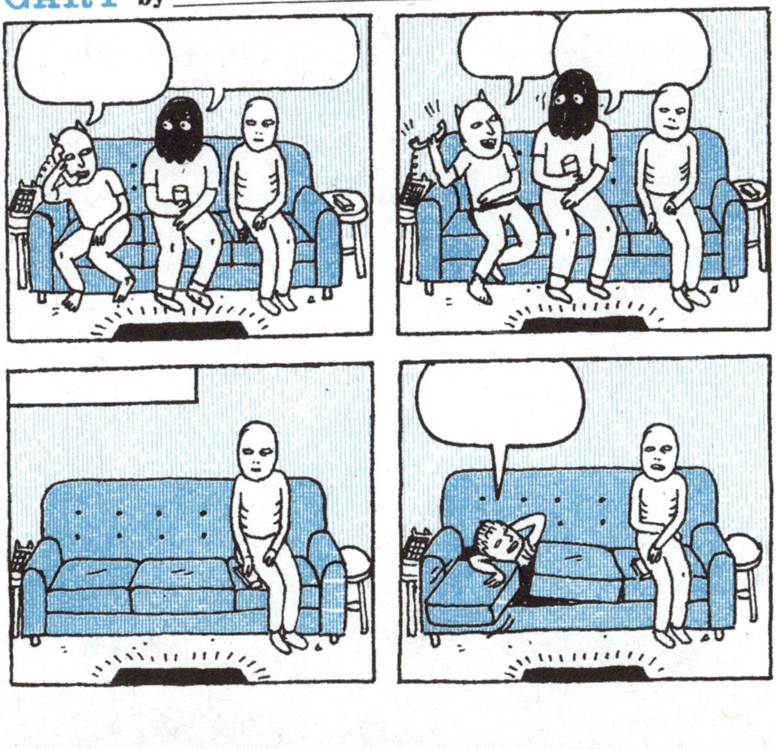

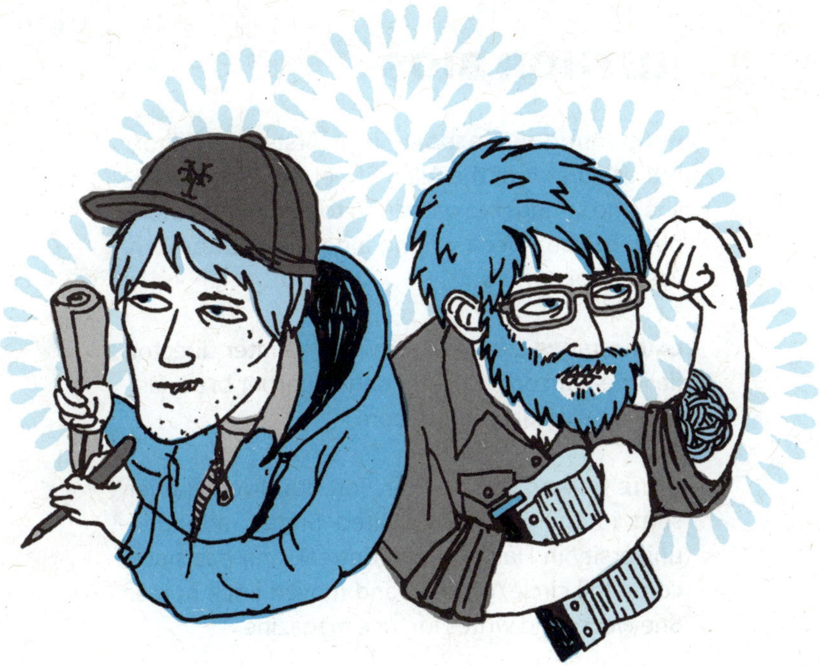

YORODEO is the Halifax-based screen-printing art duo Seth Smith and Paul Hammond. The two partnered in 2003 to design and create screen-printed show posters for local events. Over the last 7 years they have focused their energy on fine art prints and posters, among other projects. They draw inspiration from comic books, science fiction, fantasy and unintentional mistakes. Their work fuses collage, doodles, meticulous illustration, pattern and texture.

AUTHOR BIOS

JENNER-BROOKE BERGER is a first-time editor, but as curator of the Allan Street Reading Series, she's no stranger to gathering together incredible people. She's been writing a novel about broken vessels for a while.

LAURA DAWE screenwriter writer painter director flailer eater cooker poster dance-partier breakfast burrito. www.lauradawe.com

KATIE HEINDL was born in Toronto, lived a brief stint in the Southern United States, attended university in Halifax and Montréal, and has since come full circle/given in and moved back home. She works and writes for Vice magazine.

SCOTT HERDER is a writer and a musician. He currently lives in Guelph, where he is a graduate student, and where he often walks his puppy, Pascal.

ANDREW HOOD's book, *Pardon Our Monsters*, received the 2008 Danuta Gleed Award for best first collection of short stories in English. He's at work (maybe right as you read this) on a novel about treasure hunting.

MINDY HUNG is a New York-based Canadian writer. Her fiction has appeared or is forthcoming in *Halfway Down the Stairs*, *Grain*, and *PANK*. Her non-fiction has been published in *The Walrus*, *Salon*, and *The New York Times*. She is a 2010 fellow in Fiction from the New York Foundation for the Arts.

GEORDIE MILLER is a graduate student in English at Dalhousie University. When he grows up, he wants to live in a tenured utopia where he discusses books and ideas all day. His work has been featured in comedy clubs, back drawers, Allan Street living rooms, grad bars, clandestine notebooks, class anthologies, and his mother's best hopes.

BEN STEPHENSON is a person from New Brunswick who doesn't live in New Brunswick anymore. His first name means "Son of My Right Hand." His right hand has a son, too. It's a little tiny hand the size of an average fingernail that edits his writing for him with a tiny pencil.

JOSHUA TIBBETTS resides in Halifax. This is his only published fiction as of the writing of this bio, but as of the publishing of this book, perhaps there are others, if he should be so lucky. He is currently attempting to get his novel *Tiny Little Oswalds* published, unless it is now published. If so, please buy multiple copies.

TERI VLASSOPOULOS lives and writes in Montréal. Her first collection of short stories, *Bats or Swallows*, will be published by Invisible Publishing in the fall. Her non-fiction has been included in the anthologies *The Art of Trespassing* (Invisible Publishing) and *She's Shameless: Women write about growing up, rocking out and fighting back* (Tightrope Books). She has also been making zines for over 10 years.

INVISIBLE PUBLISHING is committed to working with writers who might not ordinarily be published and distributed commercially. We work exclusively with emerging and under-published authors to produce entertaining, affordable books.

We believe that books are meant to be enjoyed by everyone and that sharing our stories is important. In an effort to ensure that books never become a luxury, we do all that we can to make our books more accessible.

We are collectively organized and our production processes are transparent. At Invisible, publishers and authors recognize a commitment to one another, and to the development of communities which can sustain and encourage storytellers.

If you'd like to know more please get in touch.
info@invisiblepublishing.com

Invisible Publishing
Halifax & Toronto

TO DO:
STUFF TO DO

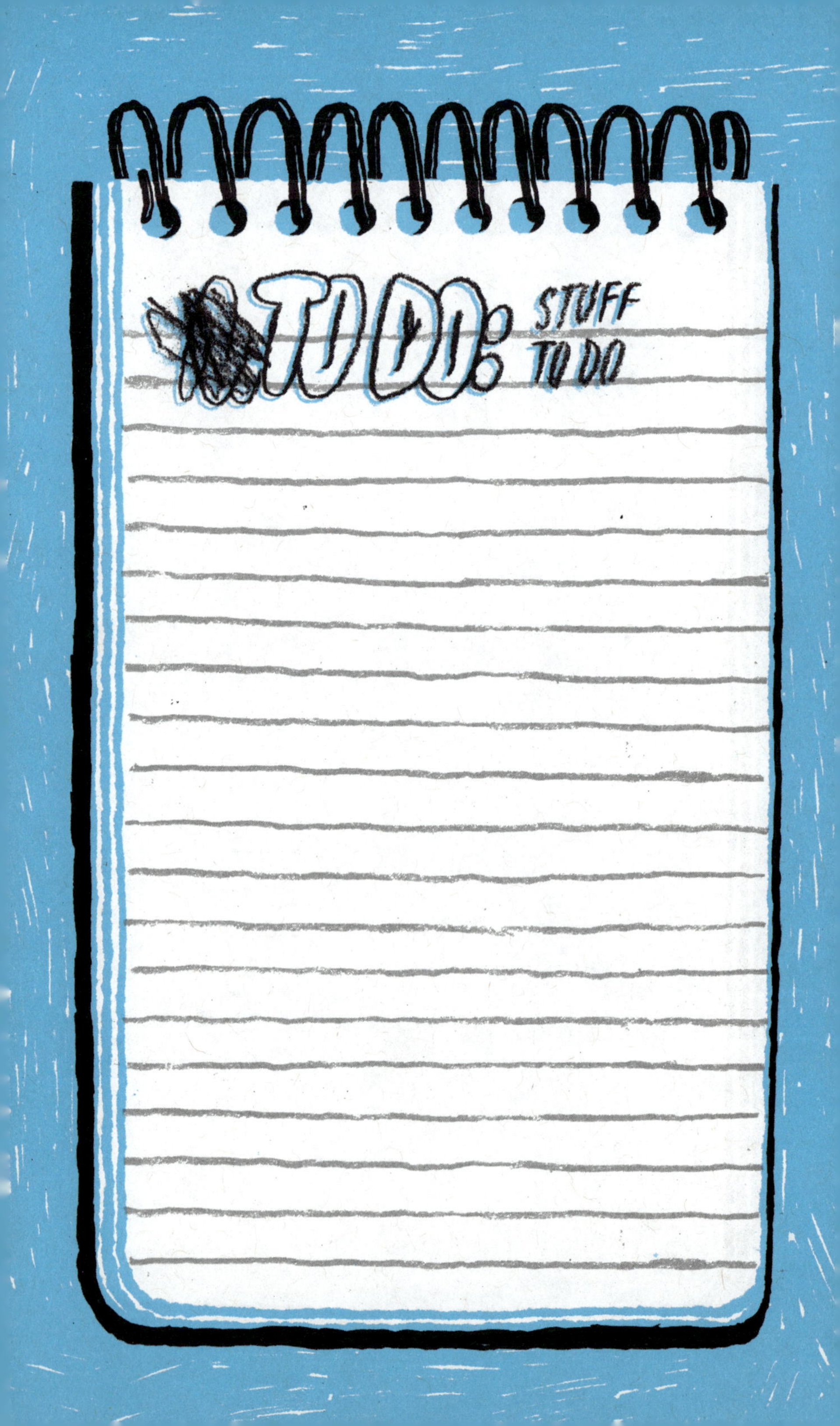
TO DO:
STUFF TO DO